"I'm not the big bad wolf," Tom said.

He slid closer to Blythe. As if she wasn't already too aware of his presence, wasn't already undergoing overheated longings.

"I'm Tom," he murmured. "The guy who loved you from the time you were fifteen."

"Somewhere behind baseball and ranching and a little number named Dana," Blythe retorted, "You're the yo-yo who called my car my best feature."

"If I've made you bitter, I'm sorry."

"Don't flatter yourself," Blyth̶ ̶ ossed back. "I wouldn't wish young lo̶ ̶ ̶ ̶ne."

"You *are* bitter"̶ ̶ ̶ ̶ ̶d. "I'm sorry." A broad fi̶ ̶ ̶ ̶ ̶arlobe. He starte̶

"You̶ ̶ ̶ ̶ ̶ed her moist cheek, taking ̶ ̶ ̶ ̶gue. "I promise you, you'll ne̶ ̶ ̶ ̶her tear over me. Forever. For always."

Promises…

Dear Reader,

What would July be without fun in the sun, dazzling fireworks displays—or heartwarming love stories from the Special Edition line? Romance seems even more irresistible in the balmy days of summer, and our six books for this month are sure to provide hours of reading pleasure.

This July, Myrna Temte continues her HEARTS OF WYOMING series with an engaging story about best friends turned lovers. THAT SPECIAL WOMAN! Alexandra McBride Talbot is determined not to get involved with her handsome next-door neighbor, but he goes to extraordinary lengths to win this single mom's stubborn heart in *Urban Cowboy*.

Sometimes true love knows no rhyme or reason. Take for instance the headstrong heroine in *Hannah and the Hellion* by Christine Flynn. Everyone warned this sweetheart away from the resident outcast, but she refused to abandon the rogue of her dreams. Or check out the romance-minded rancher who's driven to claim the heart of his childhood crush in *The Cowboy's Ideal Wife* by bestselling author Victoria Pade—the next installment in her popular A RANCHING FAMILY series. And Martha Hix's transformation story proves how love can give a gruff, emotionally scarred hero a new lease on life in *Terrific Tom*.

Rounding off the month, we've got *The Sheik's Mistress* by Brittany Young—a forbidden-love saga about a soon-to-be betrothed sheik and a feisty American beauty. And pure, platonic friendship turns into something far greater in *Baby Starts the Wedding March* by Amy Frazier.

I hope you enjoy each and every story to come!

Sincerely,

Tara Gavin,
Editorial Manager

Please address questions and book requests to:
Silhouette Reader Service
U.S.: 3010 Walden Ave., P.O. Box 1325, Buffalo, NY 14269
Canadian: P.O. Box 609, Fort Erie, Ont. L2A 5X3

MARTHA HIX

TERRIFIC TOM

Silhouette ®

SPECIAL EDITION ®

Published by Silhouette Books

America's Publisher of Contemporary Romance

To each woman
whose cheekbones aren't etched
whose behind isn't boyish
yet finds happiness in herself despite it all
and to the flawed yet terrific man
who loves her

With special thanks to Christine Armstrong, R.N.,
an inspiration to us all

 SILHOUETTE BOOKS

ISBN 0-373-24186-0

TERRIFIC TOM

Copyright © 1998 by Martha Hix

This edition published by arrangement with Harlequin Books S.A.

® and TM are trademarks of Harlequin Books S.A., used under license.
Trademarks indicated with ® are registered in the United States Patent
and Trademark Office, the Canadian Trade Marks Office and in other
countries.

Printed in U.S.A.

Books by Martha Hix

Silhouette Special Edition

Every Moment Counts #344
What To Do About Baby #1093
Terrific Tom #1186

Silhouette Romance

Texas Tycoon #779

MARTHA HIX

and her husband live in Texas, where they have reared daughters, raised hell and had a heck of a lot of fun doing both. Traveling the earth and the Internet, cheering on her favorite NBA teams and doting on her toddler grandkids are Martha's favorite pastimes. This award-winning author has written numerous historical and contemporary romance novels.

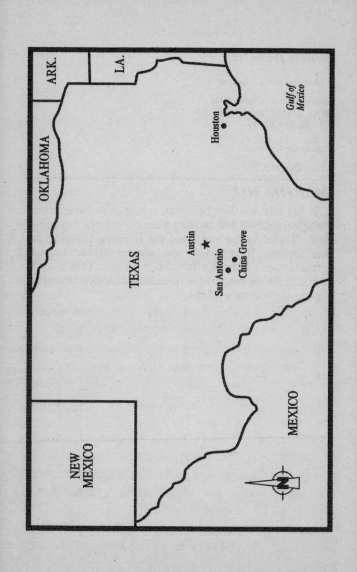

Chapter One

Before this twilit moment Blythe Redd rated buying into an Egyptian body wrap to lose weight as the stupidest thing she'd ever done in her thirty-two years. Not so. Calling on her former high-school sweetheart at the leavings of his Texas ranch? More than stupid. Bearing no likeness to Tom Terrific of fifteen years past, he was now on the attack.

A whole pecan whizzed by her. Another salvo nearly smacked the straw hat she'd paid a king's ransom for in a moment of monetary insanity. The yapping Pomeranian in her care, all nine pounds of him, yanked at his leash, ready for vengeance.

"Get out of my yard," Tom Tillman bellowed, mooselike. "Take that dog to your hot-shot red car, and haul it!"

Sourpuss. "I traveled cross-country to see you. And what do I get?"

She had her reasons for this visit. See Tom, let him know scars needn't mark the end of his world.

Her main reason? The dog's owner had written to say Tom needed help. Who better to give it than an old flame? Twice today, Blythe had tried to phone Sweet Creek Ranch. Twice, she got a grouchy recording. Both times she'd left a cheery message.

She would say her piece before twilight deepened. "I hear you stay in a lousy mood." Her hoop earrings bobbed as she spoke. "But this thing with the pecans stinks."

He retreated behind beat-up bamboo shades; they hung askew from porch rafters, resembling lines of Third World laundry. "Redd, I told you to stay back, or I'd make you."

"I'm not hawking aluminum siding or carpet cleaning. Although from the looks of it, this place could use some siding. A potted plant here and there wouldn't hurt, either."

"Dammit," he bellowed. "Leave me alone. I've got enough trouble without your adding to it."

"There is that."

She glanced to the right, in the creek's direction, where a copse of trees formed a backdrop to the decaying barn and stable. Tom and his ranch had really taken a nosedive. Was there a sunny side to this? The trees appeared sturdy. And while he might be twenty or so pounds thinner than she recalled, Tom didn't appear on the verge of starvation.

Blythe understood his nosedive, given the situation,

but things could change, as would this day soon become night. Raring for change, she announced sunnily, "This is a fine June evening to renew old acquaintances."

"Yeah, Big Redd. It's dandy," Tom said, the scathe in his tone scorching her eardrums.

"Big Redd. That's a new one from you. Ridicule." An unkind classmate had coined the popular *Big* Redd nickname during their sophomore year of high school, yet Tom had always made her feel better about her physique. "You always corrected anyone who called me names."

"Things change."

How true.

She might have arrived with noble purpose, but down deep she'd held a *slight* dream that bells would ring, birds would sing and he'd yank her into his arms while crooning, "I was such a fool to let you go."

Thank goodness her romantic fantasy hadn't included Wagnerian processionals or honeymoons in Bora Bora. In reality she needed a quick fix. To erase him from her mind. After crepe paper wilted at their upcoming high-school reunion, she would return to the real world, the past finally put to rest.

Boy, talk about a plan working, and quicklike. Who needs this aggravation? This is the pits. Just like when she gave her virginity, only to have him steal her innocence.

She whispered softly so he couldn't hear her, "Maybe I fooled myself, thinking there's still something good in you. No. I'm not a fool. Stupid, maybe. But no fool." Maybe.

And Blythe took notice—he didn't lob more pecans.

Tucking Nippy in an arm also holding her handbag, she marched through the flowerless yard to the four steps below the rundown frame house, where Tom hovered in shadows, turning his back to her. "I haven't seen you in fifteen years. I—"

"Don't come any closer, Redd. I know why you're here. Curiosity. Pity. Go back where you came from."

"You really have changed." She wished for a clear look at the blond Adonis of old, yet dreaded it at the same time. A selfless act of heroism two years past, she'd been told upon arrival in China Grove, had done serious damage to his person.

"Not only did you correct unkind classmates, you used to say sweet things to me," she noted. "You made me feel like I could conquer the world."

From the safety of the porch, he faced her. "You deserved it."

Aha! Her first ray of hope. Since the sun had fallen over the western horizon, and with Tom's long-suffering grandmother sure to return home soon, Blythe had to work fast. She inched closer to her first love.

He backed up.

Nippy growled.

Her sunglasses, coupled with the Palm Beach, four-hundred-dollar chapeau—a reasonable facsimile of which, she'd discovered this afternoon, could be had for ten bucks at discount stores—darkened too much of Blythe's vision. She hooked one temple of the shades inside the neck of her low-cut blouse.

Tom drawled, "That's quite a getup. Gypsy earrings, wild colors. Looks gr—"

Gross? He had, after all, called her big. Why wouldn't he further insult her?

As for the earrings, they were a gift from her dear, departed mother-in-law. Blythe loved these fun hoops; her usual garb consisted of a drab uniform.

Recalling his ill-fitting jeans and long-sleeved shirt not making much of a fashion statement, she glanced at her splashy printed top. "I travel light. Bought this outfit today—I thought you liked bright colors."

"You look fine."

"That's a relief. Tom, I understand you don't like visit—"

Nippy began to wiggle. She would have preferred to make this visit without the snippy Pomeranian, but she'd agreed to dog-sit for Margaret Saldivar, Nippy being too spoiled to be left alone.

"I know you don't like visitors," Blythe finished saying, losing control of her wiggling charge. Her handbag slipped. She left the clutch on the ground. "Margaret—"

"Has a mouth like the Grand Canyon. Take that dog and go!"

"You like dogs. You know you do." Once, a prized border collie worked the rich South Texas pastures with him. Man and dog, at one with their duties. Even when Tom took to the local baseball diamond, Snip had waited in the dugout, with his pink tongue lolled in devotion. "This is Margaret's little Nippy."

Nippy bared his teeth.

"I don't like anything," Tom claimed. "Especially meddling women and silly dogs."

"I am a buttinsky. I traveled from Florida to meddle."

She smiled. "Not once did I get a speeding ticket on the drive here."

"Take one step onto this porch, and you'll get a pecan between the eyes."

His aim wasn't up to his baseball-pitching days. The pecan salvos proved that. None had cold-cocked her. Why be sadistic and mention his faded glory? Besides she knew Tom was making idle threats. "You don't hit women. You're a good guy. You volunteered in the community, were a great neighbor. Margaret says you sang in the church choir and never once lost patience with screech-voiced old lady Packard."

"She was my second-grade teacher. You don't bawl out your second-grade teacher. It's un-American."

"You probably kissed babies." Should she mention the part about his charging into a blazing mobile home to rescue a pair of young sisters?

"Guys like you wear white hats." One sandaled foot on a porch step, she grasped Nippy tighter and took hold of the remarkably sturdy railing. "You're crotchety, but you don't hit women."

"Redd, dammit, not another step closer! Or else—"

She climbed. Suddenly pain exploded on the side of her nose, stunning her. She lost her footing; her grip loosened. A tornado of russet fur swirled, as did Blythe's sunglasses and Palm Beach hat. Flying backward, she screamed, hitting the ground, the air knocked from her lungs, the dog beneath her.

As if from a far distance, she heard canine howls.

"You'll squash that mutt," Tom roared, although Blythe barely heard him. "Roll off him, Redd!"

Too disoriented to think, much less act, she lay inert,

staring walleyed at the purple sky. A tall man crouched over her, his overlong hair curtaining his face. Tom.

"You tried to kill me," Blythe charged, having built lung power. "You're nasty. Hateful. You could have killed Nippy."

"Not a bad idea about Nippy. But I'm sorry about hitting you. I aimed for the dog. Honestly."

"Wow, you are a hero."

"Can't help the way I am. And the pecans were handy."

"What a guy."

He grasped her shoulder, gave it a yank and freed the Pom, who lunged to sink fangs into his rescuer's right wrist. This time Tom howled.

Blythe shoved an elbow into the ground and got to a seated position; Tom tried to shake off his attacker. "No, Nippy," she ordered. "No, no!"

The Pomeranian not only refused to obey, he sank those fangs deeper. The ball of fur waved; Tom continued to bellow. Blythe lumbered to stand and grabbed the leash before clamping the scruff of Nippy's neck. "Bad dog!"

"It's okay, little fellow." As if touched by magic, Tom's drawl now had a Texas-style croon in it. "That's it. Be a good boy."

Nippy eased down.

Just like when he was a teenager and every dog in China Grove was panting after him—every girl in high school, too—Tom had turned terrific. "Redd?"

She noted the concerned pitch to his voice, and took that as another good sign, especially when he added, "Are you okay?"

"Takes more than a fall to whip *Big Redd*."

"You probably need an ice pack for that eye."

While the dim light and his mop of hair precluded getting a good eyeful of Tom, she noted that his shoulders were still wide, his stomach still flat and he hadn't shrunk. As always, she had to tap up her chin for an eye-to-eye. He appeared in fair shape from his two-year recuperation, after saving those little girls.

She couldn't tell for sure. But at least he had hair.

He teetered backward, without his former grace. Big deal. He hadn't been a kid since E.T. phoned home. Yet, for his sake, she wished he were the same old Tom. A smile on his handsome face and an easy laugh on his lips, even if they went along with lying about what could have been their future.

"Come in the house," he said. "I'll fix you a glass of tea, too. Granny Myrt's strawberry tea."

Blythe smiled. A word with Tom Tillman—exactly what she'd asked for. Getting hit by a pecan, falling off a porch and suffering a rebuff? Worthwhile endeavors. It might even be worth suffering strawberry tea.

"What about Nippy?" she asked.

"I think I still have a box of dog biscuits. Somewhere."

He'd asked her in. Dumb thing, that. Forever had passed since Tom Tillman invited anyone into his home.

He'd spent two interminable years of self-imposed isolation, watching TV, mourning his losses and pondering the question: if he had it to do over again, would he have made a third trip into that burning trailer house?

All of which had made a beast out of him. On the

heels of selling livestock and extra land, he'd even sent his dog away, along with his wife, the latter more than ready to go.

He didn't want Blythe in the place where he hid from the world, this redhead with eyes as large as her heart. But fate could be cruel. Here she was, more attractive than ever, her perfume promising erotic excitement, melding with the memory-provoking fragrance of Blythe alone.

Often in the years after her army-man father departed Fort Sam Houston, taking his family to Germany, Tom would have loved seeing her. She'd been the home run in a batting-a-hundred life.

Tom just didn't want her to see him.

Not like this.

Too late for turning back, though. By the dim glow of a night lamp in what Granny Myrt called the parlor, he put down a newly emptied box of dog biscuits to rub the dog bites dotting the scar tissue on his wrist. His eyes accustomed to being in the dark, he studied the girl he'd once loved. The sweetheart who'd given the precious gift of allowing him to be her first man, then broken his heart by going away.

The woman who knew how to cause a stir filled his grandmother's chair, the promised ice pack covering half her face. The five-ten, robust teen had once hidden her slightly top-heavy shape behind drab, sacklike dresses that skimmed her ankles. The zaftig woman she'd turned into dressed to draw attention. She wore capri pants and a blouse in his favorite primary colors, the scooped neck of that blouse showing smooth skin and her bustline, both of which he'd always admired.

Still a lot of woman, Blythe Redd. But to his way of thinking, bones were for dogs, meat for man.

Tom made a neutral remark. "Dog's asleep, I see."

She lowered the ice pack, giving him a glimpse of her second best feature, eyes as green as cottonwood leaves waving beneath a summer sky. "How can you see anything?" she asked.

He saw something, all right. Diamonds—large diamonds in a band of gold—circled her ring finger. Some rich guy had made her his wife. A rush of jealousy snaked up his spine.

"You have this room too dark," she said.

Did she have a family? He shoved away curiosity to reply, "You know why. Don't play games."

"We're all scarred. Everyone lugs extra baggage. Some people have a hard time dealing with it."

This Goody Two-shoes outlook of hers didn't change his mind about liking her transformation in style, but it roused his anger. "I've heard stuff like yours too often. First in the hospital, then from nosy neighbors when they showed up, uninvited and unannounced. Before I barred the door."

"Maybe they were right."

Seeking to bring her down, he voiced the sort of cruelty he'd never uttered as a kid. "You'd know about baggage, wouldn't you, Big Redd? You never got your weight under control."

"That's right. I haven't. I'm a size sixteen." She grinned. "Okay, eighteen."

What would it take to hurt her, to send her away from the Sweet Creek? He wanted nothing more, besides the impossible dream of being whole again, than for Blythe

Redd to leave. Whatever it took—fine! He was a beast, and knew it.

He turned toward a window, one of several with shades drawn, day and night. "You got business in China Grove? If that business is me, move on."

"Why are you acting naive? You know our high-school reunion is coming up. I wouldn't miss it for the world."

"That's a fool thing." He shook his head, incredulous yet unconvinced she'd traveled from wherever to look a few old schoolmates in the eye. The beast reared its head. "Why ask for a snubbing? Everyone made it rough for you. With the exception of your girlfriend, Margaret."

"Oh? What about you?" A look he well remembered spilled over Blythe's round face. She twirled a curl.

Her hair *used* to be a long titian mane, her third best feature. She must have come straight from the Woof Clipper grooming salon. Well, it didn't look bad. Her curls were soft. Even if her hair was shorter than his own, Tom liked the new look. He found it easier to see just how pretty she'd become.

"I'm waiting, Tom. What about you?"

He wouldn't get into that. "If you're here to talk me into attending the reunion, forget it. You're wasting your time."

"You may change your mind. And I won't waste time. It's too precious." To make her point she jabbed a forefinger.

Her cardinal-red nailpolish reminded him of the paint on the sports car she'd driven up the dirt-and-gravel path to his house. Her fingernails weren't long; those weren't a layabout's hands. She'd always had pretty hands, no matter the condition.

"I'm determined not to waste my time with you," she said. "I could have stayed at my Florida condo, of course. I'd been savoring a respite from my career, enjoying my elderly neighbors. Then a notice arrived from the tracking service hired by the reunion organizer."

"Ron Dinlum," Tom put in.

She went on. "I threw the notice away. Wasn't interested in the alumni of our school. A week later a letter arrived from Margaret Saldivar. She urged me to attend the reunion, offered the hospitality of the Saldivar home. She also mentioned you lead a life too quiet, after suffering a grievous blow."

Tom's muscles went rigid. "You *are* here for pity."

"I didn't study my reasons. Didn't give thought to what I'd do between now and the reunion if you wouldn't welcome me. I checked the car's tires and changed the oil. It didn't take ten minutes to pack my duffel bag and head west."

"What did the hubby and kiddies say about that?"

"Nothing. And don't twist the issue. I'd like a welcome."

She'd skated over the family issue, he noticed. If she wasn't concerned over the little man and the rugrats, why should Tom be? Not that easily swayed from right, yet weakening as he considered her efforts of this day, he replied, "We don't always get what we want."

Her gaze slanted in disappointment. "Maybe I am wasting time. Like I used to, when I wouldn't listen to your advice. Remember what you always told me?"

"I remember. If you can't change the way you look, change the way you think."

"Exactly." She nodded once. "I got wise at university. Before that, I made myself miserable, dieting to try to become a clone of girls like Dana McCabe."

Dana. Blythe must know he'd married the brat, three months after graduation. Why wouldn't she know? Margaret did have a Grand Canyon mouth.

"One day," Blythe said, "I asked myself, 'Where am I going, what am I doing and what have I accomplished?' That's when I decided to do as you suggested. It changed my life."

"Congratulations, Redd. You've made a success."

"Success could be yours, too."

"You end up a preacher?" he asked, newly defensive.

"I did not."

What had she ended up? University, Florida, condo, respite. What did it add to? *Forget it.* But he wondered just how married she was, and decided: not much.

Blythe stood—to leave? An ache went through him, a hurt that tongued like flashover flames. If he let her go a second time— *No!* He had to let her go, married or not.

She looked him in the eye to say, "You've got blood on the cuff of your shirt. I think I better return the favor and see to your wounds. I'm trained in these things."

She snapped on the table lamp. Her eyes widened.

He cringed, turned sideways. His good hand went to the neck of his top-buttoned shirt to shield his throat. He couldn't help it.

"You don't look bad," she blurted.

"You lie."

Without breaking stride, she asked, "Does Myrtle still keep her first-aid supplies in the bathroom cabinet?"

"She does."

"I'm going to tend your wounds. If you'll let me."

Damn her. Damn Blythe Redd—or whatever her name had changed to. She bore down like a herd of stampeding cattle. It took an awful lot for Tom to form a simple answer, but some strange urge forced him to answer simply, "If you must."

As she riffled through the Tillman medicine cabinet, Blythe muttered, "Sheesh." Margaret had mentioned scars, but how dare he become a hermit—over no more than a few flaws on his neck and jaw?

I've seen worse. I've seen arms gone, legs gone, heads gone. I've seen children— My own husband... Tom, you could be much worse off!

Setting a roll of gauze on the vanity counter, she grumbled, "That's the thing with pretty people. They get a pimple, and think they'll never be asked to the dance again."

She scrubbed her hands with soap, and gave silent thanks for having soap. Many times she'd gone wanting simple antiseptics. "Okay, he's scarred, but the ugly part is his attitude."

Yes, but he had softened enough to invite her in for an ice pack. Hey, that beat pecan rockets and "Get off my porch." And what about old lady Packard?

Still and all, if Blythe were smart, she'd collect Nippy and scat. Sure, she could leave. And go home to what? No man, no kids, not even a house cat.

Someday, maybe soon, she'd return to her overseas

career, where misfortune's children not only needed her, but also appreciated her efforts. She ought to be resting up for that. "I don't need rest. I'm fit as a fiddle!"

She gathered tubes and supplies into the tuck of her arm and set a standing-tall course for Tom Tillman.

Again, the lights were dim in the front room. This time she wouldn't turn on the lamp. It didn't take much light to see the red blink of the telephone answering machine. Apparently he hadn't heard her messages. She recognized the same TV she'd watched as a teenager, the same old furniture and tables. The sole sound? The drone of a window-unit air conditioner. She did note a bare space. Once a record player had been in the corner. A record player to play the old tunes that she and Tom had danced to. So much for record players.

This was what the French called *un trou*. A dreary hovel. She'd seen snazzier houses in Sarajevo.

Sprucing up could make a difference, though. And the plumbing worked. It could be worse. "Nice place."

Tom made some sort of sound, akin to the growl of a beast on the African veld. He slouched in the recliner, near the chair Blythe previously occupied, and stared at the TV's black screen. Nippy, with what appeared to be a canine grin of contentment, lay curled in his lap. Indeed, Tom hadn't lost his touch with dogs.

Blythe set the Pom to his paws and tapped him out of the way with the toe of her sandal. She knelt next to Tom. "I need to roll up your sleeve."

"I don't suppose you'd take no for an answer."

"You remember I'm stubborn."

He gave a soft yet mirthless chuckle. A sneer? "Yeah, Redd. I remember all about you."

What did he mean? Better not to ask.

She remembered...remembered a young man who'd been pleasant and playful, yet sometimes gloomy. What a tragedy, gloom taking over.

Wordlessly, she unbuttoned his shirt cuff and rolled it halfway up his forearm. Even by the dim glow of the night-light, she could see what being a hero had cost him.

His right hand had pitched many innings, had once reigned reins while roping cattle. That palm was the first to caress her intimately. And if she'd had her way, it would have been the last.

His flesh bore the scars of heroism. Skin grafts and patterns of drawn, whitened epidermis spread above the rolled edge of his sleeve. How far did they spread? One could survive okay with healed burns, if the vital organs—

"Were your lungs or heart damaged? I asked Margaret—she didn't think so. I'd like to know for sure."

"I'm bleeding, and you ask about my heart and lungs?"

Glancing at his new injury, she winced, but he did answer her question. "My ticker and lungs are fine."

"That's good to hear." Her mind eased at his prospects for longevity, she examined his immediate problem. As surely as despots overpowered peasants in underdeveloped nations, these puncture wounds had to hurt tender flesh. *Detach. Act as if he's no more than a nameless patient.*

"Are you current on your tetanus inoculation?" At his nod, she said, "Good. These bites aren't serious. I checked Nippy's collar. He's had his shots."

"Whoop-de-do."

"I'll bathe your wounds, slather on antiseptic ointment and wrap your wrist in gauze." She did. "You'll be fine in a few days. Take some aspirin if it hurts."

"And call you in the morning, Ms. Doctor? Forget it. You've eyeballed the town freak." He drew back his arm, dismissing her. "Let's call it a night. Just say goodbye. Like we did after graduation."

Their goodbye. A claw of memory dug into her. "I recall two goodbyes. One at the air base." Where Tom had promised a future. "Or do you refer to the previous evening, on the banks of Sweet Creek?" The last of many beautiful evenings.

"I refer to a clean break." His jaw ticked. "Goodbye, good luck."

"Sayonara," she muttered.

"Grow up, Blythe Redd. We're not kids anymore. Teenage infatuation won't happen again."

"Grow up? Maybe I should. I've waved adieu to thirty. Maybe I ought to be clever enough to know you didn't mean your youthful declarations of love. What a downer, growing up."

His eyes softened with sadness, he said, "Yeah, Redd. You're right. Growing up is a downer."

"I'm glad you didn't say we're too old for love, when we haven't even reached thirty-five." She unfurled his cuff. "Why, I'm looking forward to fat and forty."

Too often she'd witnessed people, even loved ones, fall short of forty. Or thirty. Or ten. "Old age will be nice, too. That's neither here nor there. This is here, this is now."

She canted close enough to feel the heat of his body

and to smell the male scent of him. He might be doing everything in his power to reject her, but why not make him squirm? "Come on, sourpuss. What would be wrong with the tiniest kiss, to refresh our memories? A peck on the lips between consenting adults."

Sadness vanished; his blue eyes rounded. "You're nuts. Barging in here, taking charge, wanting kisses. Pathetic."

"I don't have to take this abuse. Besides, who's the wacked one here? I'm not the one holed up in a darkened house, striking out at friendship."

His left hand snaked behind her neck. Fingers digging into her nape, he said, "Don't push things. Let it go. Let it alone. Do the reunion thing, if you must, then go back where you came from. But keep your distance while you're in the vicinity."

Studying the angular planes of Tom's wounded yet still appealing face, she knew she could cry uncle and be on her way. Nope. Not without another try at getting to him. Her mouth pursed in exaggeration. "Want to see my Madonna impersonation?"

"No," he answered and removed his fingers from her nape.

Did he try to hide a grin? She suspected so. Testing him, she asked, "How about I show you my—?"

"How about you don't."

Okay, no grin. He'd lost his sense of humor, too. Snapping her fingers, she wouldn't give in quite yet. "This place could use some livening up. Tell you what. My neighbor in Florida, Mirtika Mezkat, taught me the macarena. If you hum, I'll dance."

Nippy reared his head and whined once.

"Take the dog's advice, Redd. Don't."

Okay. A *serious* try. "Swallow a healthy dose of reason, Tom Tillman. I'm fat and you've been burned. We're apt to stay that way. So what? Doesn't make us evil."

"You don't understand," he said quietly. "My life is over."

"A cyclops couldn't be as far removed as you are from Terrific Tom of old." Affixing the top on the tube of ointment, she added, "You live in the most secure country on this earth. And—"

"Excuse me?" He cocked his head, shook it in disgust. "You never heard of drive-by shootings?"

"You have a home."

"It's a dump."

"Elbow grease and a whole lot of 'out of chair, onto feet' would help. I hear you don't even make a living anymore."

"I don't need to. I've got money."

"So I hear. Margaret clued me in to your fattened purse. Came from land sales and a hefty out-of-court settlement, she says. What blessings. Money, and plenty to eat."

He curled his lip; his were a fine set of lips, despite his current expression. He still had a sexy mouth.

"Yeah on the eats," he said. "So do you."

"I look on a hot meal as a blessing." Many times, her food had been freeze-dried or cold, or nonexistent. Tom not being into blessings, she moved the emphasis to him. "Myrtle Tillman waits on you like a servant."

"She's my granny. She wants to do for me."

"I guess you could do worse."

"Yeah, Redd. I could end up at our reunion."

"That does it. You wear 'poor me' like cheap cologne. I don't like stinky stuff. Nipster, let's go."

"Finally." Tom scooped Nippy up with his good hand, made for the front door and deposited the Pomeranian on the other side of it, even though the dog attempted to stay. "'Bye."

"*Sayonara,* sourpuss." She breezed by the fallen hero, but slowed. "If you've got brain one, you'll cease feeling sorry for yourself. Quit letting your grandmother take care of you. You could become an inspiration to other burn victims. Be the old Tom Tillman. Terrific."

"Fat chance."

Chapter Two

Blythe Redd marched hotly from Tom Tillman's porch into the night, dragging a reluctant dog behind her. The Pom didn't want to leave. "Too bad, Nippy. Ours is not to reason why."

Blythe snapped up her spilled belongings, and made a beeline for her car. After punching the remote button for the electric door lock and shoving her stuff and Margaret's pet inside, she heard a motor and saw a set of headlights. They came from a pickup truck kicking gravel in its noisy wake; it plowed toward her.

The pickup skidded to a stop so fast that the rear end fishtailed. With a squeak the driver-side door belched open; a white-haired woman shot from the interior, both hands together, lifted and pointed toward Blythe.

"I've got a gun, thief!" came the high-pitched country drawl of Myrtle Tillman. "Hands up, or else I'll shoot!"

"No need for that, Myrtle. It's Blythe Redd. Remember me?"

The arms lowered. "Rock 'n' roll!"

Blythe wondered if she'd heard right. Slang out of a woman over seventy? Well, Myrtle had always been young—and wild—at heart.

"Honey girl, what're you doing in this neck of the woods?" Tom's grandmother asked.

"I came to see your grandson."

"Uh-oh." Myrtle walked closer. A head shorter than Blythe, she raised her chin. She did indeed pack a firearm.

Blythe cocked a thumb toward the Pom; he tried to scratch out the car window. "Interested in a ride? I'd like a chat."

"I've got groceries. Better put 'em away, then I'm free—if Tom don't need nothing."

Blythe's lips flattened. "He's not an invalid. Nothing says he can't do for himself."

"Guess I've babied him."

"No joke." Pivoting around, Blythe went to the car, opened the door and leaned on the horn. The calm, country night shattered. Nippy howled. Myrtle jumped. And birds, having roosted in the trees, scattered.

Tom moved onto his porch. "What's going on out there?"

"Your grandmother's got groceries. Grab them. Put them away while you're at it. Myrtle's going for a ride with me."

"Honey girl, you sure have turned bossy."

"Right." Blythe waited for Tom to comment, but he didn't. He moved toward the groceries.

"Get in, Myrtle," she instructed.

Tom's granny rounded the front bumper to scoot inside. "Nippy? That you, boy?"

Blythe ducked to the driver's seat; Nippy crawled into the passenger's lap. Myrtle placed a Beretta on the floorboard.

"Don't look at me like that, girl. I'm licensed to carry this piece. Texas law says I can."

"What joy, lawmakers arming the citizenry. I hate guns."

Ignoring that statement, Myrtle asked, "You been in town long? I ain't heard nothing 'bout you visiting. You staying with Margaret and Ed?"

"Yes. She's in San Antonio tonight, with Ed's mother."

"Prob'ly knocking herself out to please. Always does. She tell ya she adopted her sister's girl, even before she and Ed got hitched? Shelly's a delight. 'Cept for that screamin' hair. And she ain't too smart when it comes to boyfriends. You oughta see that loser she's sweet on. I'd send Icky Kuleska packin', guaranteed. But Margaret's patient as all get-out."

"Seems to me you're way too patient with Tom." Blythe thumped the steering wheel once for emphasis. "You coddle him. He needs to do things on his own. He needs to be made to move."

"Honey girl, you just don't understand."

Blythe understood, mainly from Margaret, that after Tom married, he bought his grandmother her own home in town, one she'd studded with flowers and the homey touches lacking at the ranch. Myrtle's bungalow now stood vacant, the flowers having gone to seed.

"You facilitate his withdrawal from society."

"Probably."

"Undoubtedly. Make Tom work for what he needs." Blythe put the car in gear. "Give a man a fish, and you feed him a meal. Teach a man to fish, and he can feed himself for life."

"Tom don't like to fish."

Silence followed, several long beats in length. Once six digits' worth of European engineering hummed down the paved road leading to China Grove, Myrtle spoke. "Nice Chevy. I always wanted a red car." She stroked the dash; orange fluorescence mixed with blue to glow in the interior, as if it were a cockpit. "Red cars make a statement."

"Exactly. That's why I bought it. But it's not a Chevy."

"Could've fooled me. You can't do no better than General Motors. Town ain't been the same since Ron Dinlum closed down his Chevy house and set up shop in San An-ton-ya."

Dinlum apparently did well enough to put his money behind the reunion. He'd taken charge, planned to hold the gathering in his vacant automobile agency. He'd always been a go-getter.

Myrtle said, "Hope you didn't get gypped."

For the first time tonight, Blythe laughed. It had been way too long since she'd had Myrtle Tillman, former boss, fret over her. People didn't fret over Blythe Redd. The world didn't turn that way. "Don't sweat the Porsche. I take care of myself."

Myrtle, a country beauty in her younger years, cast a sidelong glance. "You gussied up, driving a fancy Hupmobile, I guess you done good. Never did hear nothing. Figured you'd write Margaret so's she could let me know how you was."

"You didn't read my letters?" All two, before she'd given up on hearing from any member of the Tillman family. Margaret had been the one to write and mention Tom's marriage. After that, Blythe hadn't wanted to stay in touch with China Grove.

"Wanna thankee for teaching me figures," Myrtle said. "I get by. Even play dominoes."

"You promised you'd finish learning to read and write."

"Stuff happens." She shrugged. "My boy and his wife moved off to California even before Tom got hitched. Tom needed help at the home place. And with the livestock. Then...well, I been busy."

"I'm sorry to hear that." Blythe, saddened for diverted dreams, squeezed Myrtle's parched knuckles. "And I'm sorry Tom never made it to the big leagues."

"He got over it. Had to. Tom Senior and Evelyn hared off to California, leaving the ranch to their boy." She went on to say Tom's parents took up Zen.

"Too bad Tom couldn't use his baseball scholarship," Blythe commented, after listening to further explanations.

"Stuff happens," Myrtle repeated and sized her up in the waning light. "Young Tom always had an eye for red hair and a big...smile. If I've heard him say once, I've heard him say a bunch of times, 'Redd's Blue Bell ice cream in a mellorine world.'"

Blythe's fingers strangled the wheel. "Which is why he married a shapely cheerleader the September after graduation."

"There's a story to that, honey girl. One that ain't my place to yammer about."

No doubt. Margaret apparently didn't know, since she'd mentioned nothing on the subject. But she'd eased Blythe's mind: the former Dana McCabe wouldn't be at the reunion.

A wine cooler plus black coffee bought from the clerk at Fill-Er-Fast, she returned to her Porsche to hand the cool drink to Myrtle. "Your favorite. Strawberry." Blythe loathed anything strawberry, except for memories that related to this adorably kooky senior citizen. "Strawberry fields forever."

Both women chuckled. In high school, when Blythe worked as Myrtle's hired girl, they had sung that song, over and over, while cleaning house or washing clothes.

"Strawberry fields forever," Myrtle said, wistful and sad, the berry fields of her dreams having gone fallow. She twisted the cap. "Caught my breath while you was in the store. I'm wondering about you. You married?"

How nice, having an acquaintance ask after her. It hadn't escaped Blythe's notice, Tom's lack of curiosity. The small, tight hurt, suppressed throughout the evening, pricked her heart.

She sipped coffee to ignore it. "I'm not married."

"You're wearing a ring." Myrtle poured wine into the cup of her hand for Nippy to lap. "I'm suspicious. You ain't married. You're driving a slick car. You're dolled up, loud as a Tejano band. Blythe Redd, did you end up a call girl?''

She blinked, then her eyes widened. "Call girl?"

"One of them professional ladies. They make good money. Some's got sugar daddies to buy cars. They wear pretty clothes, too, just like you do. I know about these things. I watch TV. How much money do you make at it?''

While she should have been insulted, Blythe grinned. "Exactly zero. I'm not a hooker."

"You gotta be a model then. You in any magazines? Got 'em with you? Been on them fancy runways in Milan or Paris? I know about highfalutin places. I watch that fashion lady's show on the news channel, regular as taking my vitamins. I hear plus-size models is 'making a mark' in fashion.''

"I'm not a model." Blythe sighed, thinking how far her calling took her from glamour and runways.

Desperately needing Myrtle to fill in the gaps Margaret had left, she implored, "Tell me more about Tom.''

"He should've taken that scholarship. Or gone to California with his folks. Better yet, eloped to Nuevo Laredo with you." Myrtle surmised aloud, "Zen might've helped him.''

"I've known thousands of men who'd give anything to own a single cow in a peaceful land.''

"You been living in Mexico or somewhere weird like that?''

"No." Blythe had patched up wounds in Chiapas, though. Having worked in a succession of countries, she recalled the collective. Privation, desperation. Dirt, flies.

Disease and worse. Lack of water or too much of it. Mostly, too many bullets in too many bodies.

A simple woman in a complicated vehicle, Myrtle pressed the button to lower her window; Nippy lolled his head out. Peace, a happy dog—it was almost like heaven to Blythe.

"You still like chicken and dumplings?" Myrtle asked.

Was there anything more ordinary, more everyday in the country than boiled fowl and doughy goop? "They're like Sunday afternoons in the park, or unbrandied apple pie, or little kids playing sandlot ball. Blessings, to be sure."

"You be at the house, come tomorrow night. Tom likes to eat dinner about six."

Accepting would be simpleminded. Like having herself wrapped in herb-soaked rags as dirty as the backstreets of Karnak. A girl had gotten wrapped, hoping to lose inches. A woman would know better. Furthermore, Blythe could lose a healthy dose of peace of mind over chicken and dumplings.

"I'm going to pass," she answered.

Yet, as Blythe left Myrtle off at the frame house, her stomach growled for chicken and dumplings.

The smell of chicken and dumplings floated through the house. For somewhat in the neighborhood of five seconds, Tom found it strange, Granny Myrt setting the table, then ducking out the kitchen door. He knew. He knew before the old Chevy pickup roared down the road. He knew before a fancy red automobile pulled in front of the house. *I've been set up.*

Flee. *Do it!* But sunrays spiked through the edges of window shades. He didn't go out in daylight. The last time he had, he'd frightened a toddler. Desperation called for desperate measures, though. These were.

Abandoning his hat—no self-respecting Texas rancher went in public bare-headed!—Tom cleared the back door, as Blythe ascended the front porch steps.

Sunlight on his shirted shoulders for the first time in forever, he glanced up at the cloudless sky. The roasting sun, even at its wane, beat down on his hatless head and uncovered hands. They began to sting. He and the sun didn't mix.

He kept going, reached the patch of pasture where prickly pear grew, not cattle, not horses.

"Tom?"

Blythe. Of course, Blythe. Not far behind him. The music of mockingbirds and the distance peal of a country church's bells in his ears, he turned. His heart thumped.

She stood a dozen feet away. Big, tall Blythe. Her straw hat in place, she wore heels and a dress. Not an ankle-skimming kind of dress, a pretty one of fine material, in a shade of green that went well with her hair and complexion. She looked like a million dollars. Just what he needed. A million-dollar woman.

"You look pretty, Redd," he said, and wished he hadn't.

She grinned. A little. "Guess I didn't waste money at the Menger Smart Shop."

"You didn't."

"I've ruined my heels," she said. He couldn't stop the muscles that wanted to work into a grin.

"These shoes weren't made for walking pastures."

A gust of wind kicked up her hat brim; her hand lifted to keep it atop her head. He again saw a seventeen-year-old girl, waving goodbye, standing below the steps that led up to the air force transport jet. The aircraft that took her away. Away to Germany. Away to the circle of diamonds on her left hand.

Her eyes were on him, and she seemed to read his mind. "You said we'd marry, once you got started in the major leagues. You never even wrote to say 'forget it.'"

Tom ambled to her and held out a steadying arm so that she could get free of a snake hole. Her touch hurt him. His scars, of course. He didn't like to be touched, not anymore. But he realized something. He hurt because he'd hurt her.

But he wouldn't pretty up the truth. They were too far beyond being kids for games. "Dana claimed to be pregnant. Around these parts, men do the right thing at a time like that. I had a responsibility."

"Did you now?"

"I was lonely as a coyote, after you flew away." Lonely, and feeling the pressures of a ranch dropped in his lap. Dana had recognized his state, had set her sights. He'd been easy prey, a weakness that shamed him to this day. "She wasn't in the family way. And never got pregnant."

Blythe looked down her nose. "Oh?"

"We could've divorced, sure. But I didn't take divorce lightly," he added. "She was my wife." For better or for worse, mostly for worse. "We tried to make a go of it," he said, being generous to his ex. "Then...it got worse."

She sighed, the redhead who'd listened to and encouraged his dreams. Taking off her shoes, Blythe dropped them in the field. "She was your woman. I was a girl. Mostly."

Tom shoved fingertips into jeans' pockets. He studied the ground of South Texas. Texas. The place Blythe had left him, wide open to Dana McCabe.

Suddenly he wished he'd gotten on that plane with Blythe and flown away.

He raised his head. He didn't gaze upon a girl. He locked eyes with a woman. What sense he had left told him not to encourage her. He had little sense. "You're here for dinner, aren't you? What would your husband say about that?"

This time Blythe studied the ground. Tom watched her breasts heave. When she raised her head, she blinked, as if to wash a tear away. "My husband can't say anything. He's dead."

For two years, maybe longer, Tom Tillman hadn't thought too much about anyone but his own sorry self. It now occurred to him—*I'm not the only one who's lost something in life.*

"Be a shame to let good chicken and dumplings get cold," he said with a twist of lips.

"Delicious," Blythe commented and forced a bite down her throat, her appetite nil, her discomfort abundant from sitting across the table from Tom.

She dragged her gaze upward in the too dark kitchen. She wanted to see his expressions. Not as she grilled him about Dana. She'd said her piece on his ex-wife. Actually, Dana didn't pose the problem. Blythe couldn't

blame the vivacious cheerleader for going after Terrific
Tom. Girls had done that sort of thing. It was natural,
like breathing.

What pained Blythe? Terrible Tom. If he'd married
by shotgun arrangement in September, then he'd been
showing Dana the creek in early summer.

Depressing.

Apparently eating didn't rank highly with Tom, either.
He, too, toyed with his food. Dressed as yesterday, in
long sleeves with every button buttoned, he attended to
a can of beer.

He ran his thumb across the rim. "I'm sorry about
last night. I shouldn't have thrown pecans at you."

"I was trespassing, basically. Guess I'm fortunate you
didn't have Myrtle's gun. You might've shot me."

"You're wrong, Redd. I wouldn't have shot you."

"Aren't I lucky?"

"I'd say you're not. If you had luck on your side, you
wouldn't be here tonight."

"I'm lucky." She spoke from the bottom of her heart.
"I'm alive." At one point survival had been in doubt.

"I hate that in you. Cheeriness."

"Excuse me for living, I think, is the usual response
to something as asinine as that."

"Excuse me for taking a hard fall. Don't try to shame
me, Redd. It won't work. I am what I am." He rubbed
his right jaw, the one bearing scars. "I'm nothing more,
nothing less."

Her mind's eye drew old pictures. Tom on the ball
field, cheers from the crowd surrounding him. Tom being a good son to the father who'd looked on the ranch
as a burden. A strapping youth, high in the saddle of a

chestnut cutting horse, the sun making gold fire of his thick hair, Tom had worked cows, Snip the border collie alongside. She saw strong hands clutching reins, and muscled thighs capable of doing the work of reins, guiding Charger through Hereford cattle.

"Sure," she said. "You've taken a hard fall. I don't see why you can't climb back in the saddle. Thomas Tillman, where's your pride? Maybe you can't be a rancher. But you could do something, make some contribution."

"Why should I?"

"Because you can. You don't know how lucky you are."

"You spent too much time in Germany, is what I'm thinking."

"I've lived a thousand lives since Germany."

"How come you're a widow?" he asked out of the blue.

Talking past the lump that formed in her throat wasn't easy, but she did it. And, thankfully, didn't let loose with a threatening tear. "My husband died in the crossfire of battle. He was assigned to UN peace-keeping forces in Eastern Europe."

"He must've had good insurance."

"Excuse me?"

"He must've had good insurance," Tom repeated. "Soldiers don't make the kind of money that buys European motorcars."

She found his tone insulting, his sky-blue eyes emotionless. No way would she explain Jean-Pierre Ricard's inherited wealth, the money that financed his idealism and ultimate sacrifice, as well as his legacy. No way would she divulge heroism to a lapsed hero, devoid of sympathy or empathy.

Dedication to whatever made a man most terrific—this she found appealing.

She said, "I prefer not to discuss my financial straits. Nor my husband."

Tom tipped up the can to take a long pull from it. "What do you want to talk about?"

"Brought you something. A hand exerciser. I considered buying ponytail holders. What's with the hair?"

"What's wrong with my hair?" he said, a male offended.

"Have you ever watched *Quest For Fire?*"

"That's a cheap shot, Redd."

"Whatever works. You shouldn't hide your face. You've got a nice face."

"You had your eyes examined lately?"

"Listen up, Mr. Rusted Tongued Devil. I understand Dale Carnegie's method to win friends and influence people never goes out of date. I should've bought his book for you."

"Don't buy me gifts. I don't want them. I don't want anything but to be left alone."

"Alone. Interesting concept. Why, as we speak, I can picture you in the desert, alone as you're so eager to be. I'd love to see a video of you, struggling for water and a bite to eat. Or the simple solace of a human voice."

"Sadist."

"Who, me?" Calling up wide-eyed innocence, she formed her mouth into affront. "I'm picturing your dreams fulfilled. One should be careful what he wishes for. He might get it."

She shoved her plate away, then said, "I'll get the rubber ball."

"What makes you think it'll help? You a doctor?"

"I'm a nurse."

Tom crossed his arms. "Did you join the U.S. Army like your father and his, and all your male ancestors back to the Revolution?"

"I was too fat for the army. Worked out for the best. With women taking up arms nowadays, I might've had to shoot someone. I'm a healer, not a fighter."

"Kind of figures. You put other people's feelings ahead of your own. Women like you end up nurses. Or wives. Or mothers. Guess you got two." He cocked a brow. "How about the third?"

"Like you, I don't have children. I'm not cut out for motherhood. The course of my life took me in a different direction. I planned it that way, and have no regrets."

"Not cut out for motherhood? Seems strange. Then again, a lot of things in life are strange."

"You got that right."

"So," Tom said, pulling out the rudimentary word into an accusation, "no husband, no kids. You just trek around the country, driving a flashy car and wearing look-at-me clothes? You figuring to snag another husband?"

"Do you get your jollies, antagonizing me?"

He got a nasty grin on his unblemished mouth. "You bet."

This *was* the dumbest thing she'd ever done in her life, even more stupid than that Egyptian body wrap. Jumping up, she marched barefoot to the kitchen counter, where she'd left her purse, along with the hat she'd bought on impulse in Palm Beach. She unzipped the bulging clutch and plunked a tube of hand cream on the counter. "Tell Myrtle the cream is for her."

Blythe had her fingers around the malleable ball, which she intended to lob into the trash, when she felt Tom at her back. The whole of him.

"Look, Redd. I'm sorry for hurting your feelings. I'm a beast. I know it. I don't reckon I'll change. What's it going to take for you to get that through your head?"

"I'm getting the idea."

"It doesn't have anything to do with you," he said. "It all has to do with me. Could be Granny Myrt, or your nosy pal Margaret, put you up to this mercy mission. But they don't know everything. They don't know…"

His left hand reached around Blythe. Took the purse out of her hand. Shoved it down the counter. That hand snagged her waist, bringing her against him, closely against him. The scent of soap wafted from Tom, soap and man.

Then his lips were at her neck, his breath feathering her earlobe, the ends of his hair tickling her skin. For so long, when she should have been forgetting Tom, she'd wondered if she'd feel his lips again.

"We could go back to the creek," he whispered, his voice ragged, his body trembling. "Just like old times."

She sucked in her breath as he caressed the underside of her breast. His tongue darted to the space behind her ear, drawing a shiver. "Tom," she began, but didn't know what to say, didn't want to say anything.

"I can do this all night." His hand reached for hers. "That's as far as it would go." Tom moved her hand behind her, wedging her fingers between them, placing it at his fly. "This is why, Redd. Slugger's broken. I'm not a man anymore."

And then he pitched away from her.

What a relief, seeing the last of Blythe Redd. He didn't need her hanging around, reminding him of what he couldn't do. Hell, even if he could, Tom didn't want another woman heaving at the sight of his beat-up body, like Dana had done.

No, he didn't need another rejection, especially from Blythe. He was doing fine. He could live out his days in a darkened house, with no one disrupting his routine of doing nothing.

Funny, though. As one day turned into two, and Blythe kept her distance, he kept thinking about how she had filled this house, something nice.

On the third night he didn't know what possessed him to shower or to search for the bottle of unopened aftershave that someone had brought as a get-well gift. He slapped Balkan Breeze on the unscarred part of his jaw. Combed his hair into a ponytail. Dusted off his dress Stetson and his best Western shirt and jeans. All set, he took the pickup for the drive into town.

Gratefully, he had the cloak of darkness to shield him from the curious of China Grove. He cruised by the Saldivar house, on the off chance Blythe's car would be in the one-lane driveway.

It wasn't.

He found it parked under the canopy at Dairy Divine, hugging sides with the Saldivars' old minivan. He stopped the truck across the street, killed the engine and craned his neck to see inside the drive-in's windows. There Blythe was, decked out in something smart-looking, crowding a booth with the Saldivars that included their skinny teenager.

No one else frequented the place, besides the help. What a good time they had, Saldivars and returned friend. Dammit.

The least Blythe could do was mourn what couldn't be.

"Party hearty," Tom growled.

Get out of here. That was what he'd do. He turned the key. Got no more than fifty yards. The engine sputtered, died. Another turn of the key. Nothing. He balled his left fist and banged it once against the steering column. "This is good. This is real good." He gave the engine one more chance, fruitlessly. "Granny Myrt should've filled the tank."

He shoved from the cab and made it to Fill-Er-Fast. The gasoline pumps weren't working. Tom started down the highway, his stride slow. Damn. What he wouldn't give to be able to run. He kept going. Left foot, pull. Right foot, pull. Again and again. He could do this. He could get away. Maybe.

He began to feel better about his chances, once he got a semblance of stride to his gait. But his legs hurt. So did his hips and groin. He hadn't walked anywhere in years. In spite of his assorted aches and pains, he noticed the stars looking fine. Crickets creaked, the sound also fine.

Uh-oh. He heard a car behind him. Its motor sounded too powerful to belong to anyone in China Grove.

Wuss factor kicking in, he veered down the ravine that

ran beside the highway. He got halfway to a sheltering oak when he heard the car stop and a door slam.

"You stranded?"

Weak as a kitten, inside and out, he decided nothing would be better than climbing in Blythe's car. "I'm out of gas."

"Walking's good for atrophied muscles."

He climbed the ravine, almost reaching the roadside, where Blythe stood with hands on her hips. *She's upset.* Stood to reason. He'd done everything possible to bruise her pride. Should he apologize? "I'm...out of...breath."

"You don't get enough exercise, riding a recliner or channel surfing."

"I thought you said you aren't a sadist." His pulse hammered in his ears.

"I say a lot of things."

"So do I. Too much at times. Redd, I—"

"Still want to be alone?" she interrupted.

He needed to sit down. Frankly, he wanted to be closed up with Blythe. "Give me a ride to the pickup?"

"Moderate exercise won't hurt you. And I don't pick up strangers."

"I'm not a stranger."

"Oh, really? You think about that, Tom Tillman. Think hard and strong on that."

She whirled around, moonlight illuminating the bounce of her curls and the march in her pace. A door slammed. An engine kicked in. Tires roared away. Blythe was gone, like a streak of lightning. Damn woman. What kind of nurse abandoned the feeble?

The huge, hollow ache that had caved through him

for oh, so long got bigger, yet Tom tried to make it smaller.

Didn't work.

But something did.

His resolve.

By damn, she wouldn't get away with casting him off like a discarded pup. He reversed his course. Legged it toward China Grove with more strength than he'd ever imagined he possessed.

Halfway there, he paused to ponder her accusations. She'd been right. Nothing of late in Tom Tillman resembled the boy she remembered. Moreover, being alone had turned out pretty shabby.

"Okay," he said aloud, as if speaking to Blythe. "Let's see what we can do about getting reacquainted. Once I give you hell for kicking gravel in my face."

There would be no hell to give, nor chatter leading to a reacquaintance with the chaotic redhead. The Saldivars still sat at a Dairy Divine booth, but Blythe hadn't returned. Dammit.

Tom turned up his shirt collar, walked into the hamburger haven's bright lights. "Ed, the pumps are down at Fill-Er-Fast. I'm out of gas. Would you siphon some out of your tank?"

"Tom!" The Hispanic mechanic, who traded horses to make extra money, spilled his huge cup of iced drink. "*Dios,* man, what're you doing in town?"

"Looking for Blythe Redd."

All the Saldivars grinned, except Shelly, who piped up with, "Way cool on the ponytail."

"So," Margaret said with a smile, "you're looking for Blythe. Good."

"She left me stranded on the side of the road."

"Cool. You gotta like that in Blythe."

He didn't shoot a glare at the modern-day version of Olive Oyl. Once, he'd mentored the teenager; they had been pals of a sort. Apparently Shelly Saldivar now carried a grudge over his telling Granny Myrt not to give her a summer job.

"I will see Blythe. Tonight." Tom meant business. "Ed, you going to help me get my truck started, or not?"

The sooner he got on the road, the sooner he would show Blythe Redd what he was made of.

Chapter Three

W hat a stroke of luck, something happening to his pickup, yet Blythe still found it difficult to justify why she had deserted Tom. He must be exhausted, puffing for breath. Necessity had forced her many times to leave behind men in worse shape. That was war. This was war. He needed survival lessons.

"Lesson number one," she murmured, passing the taxidermy shop and the Woof Clipper salon. How long should she give him to study his lesson?

Blythe parked in an overgrown spot near the Little League ball field. She'd waited long enough and was about to turn the ignition when she noticed his pickup barreling toward her. Aha! She had that man on the run.

Sipping bottled water, she drummed fingernails on the steering wheel, keeping her cool, even after he shoved his face inside her lowered window.

His overstimulating, spiced scent jarred remembrance, taking her back to the Emirates and the pint-size barge captain who'd tried to wow her with a gift flagon of the same odorous aftershave of Bulgarian extraction. The Iraqi hadn't known better. Tom Tillman should have.

She asked in a voice as bold as Tom's bouquet, "Lost?"

He bared his teeth. "Get out of that car."

"Your hair looks nice."

He shucked the ponytail holder. "Step out of your car."

"Are you strong enough to make me?"

"I've got Granny Myrt's bazooka."

"You're lying."

He straightened, hooked thumbs into the back pockets of his jeans. "All right. I lied. But I want you out of that car." A forefinger jerked upward. "Move it, Redd. Don't make me use up what's left of my strength." He gestured in frustration. "Dammit, woman, I'm worn out!"

"Never hurts to stretch your endurance."

"You're sadistic. Just like I said the other night, you're nuts. Plain nuts." He sagged against the roof. "You've come back to kill me. That's what you've done."

"Life doesn't seem to mean much to you."

He muttered a string of curses, then crumpled.

Oh, Lord! Blythe tried to open the door, and failed. He was lodged against it. She climbed out the passenger side, loped around the car. Automatically checked his pulse. Feeble. Cold perspiration beaded his forehead. He'd fainted.

Great, just great. She'd pushed him beyond endurance.

It would do no good to shake him or shout. Rolling him to his back, she loosened his collar, then went for her bottle of water and a wad of tissues. Phoned the Emergency Medical Service from her car. Knelt beside Tom to wipe his brow with water. She whispered, "I'm sorry I was mean to you."

An arm closed around her. "You mean it?" he said weakly.

"You big lug." She checked his pulse again. It had stabilized. "Lie quietly. E.M.S. will be here in a minute." Naturally, she got an argument. "I'm not taking any chances," she said.

A flash of teeth. A smile. Then he drawled, "You take big chances with...strangers."

"Don't make too much of it."

"Can we just relax here a minute?"

After his fainting spell, he needed rest. She sat Indianstyle to await the emergency squad. Again she noticed his aftershave. Balkan Breeze's strong clove scent stirred a gagging reflex. She covered it.

Tom rebuttoned his shirt. "Grass is nice. The stars are nice. Share them with me. Let's get to know each other again."

"You're sure about those stars?"

"I'm sure." He patted the ground. "Please?"

She stretched out. "The grass does feel soft. Ah, the stars are nice, twinkling like diamonds on black velvet."

"I hope we're not in for a chigger attack."

Recalling the mite-size warriors that plagued this part

of the country, she clicked her tongue, mostly at Tom's pessimistic outlook. "Let's take our chances."

"Deal."

The stars might be beautiful, but she closed her eyes to them, and listened to night noises and his breathing. The latter sounded even. Excellent.

Still in her nurse mode, she wondered if his impotency problem tied directly to his sourpuss attitude. Men would give up any limb, either eye, rather than lose virility.

One or two might even make a recluse out of himself over something like that.

"I've been around burn victims, Tom. From what I've seen of you and know about anatomy, and from what I've heard about the mobile home disaster, I believe it's highly unlikely you're missing male equipment."

"Damn, Redd. You trying to embarrass me, or what?"

"I'm speaking as a professional. Do you know for sure you're irrevocably damaged?"

"Yeah, I do. I'm intact. It just doesn't work."

"If there's one thing I've learned in my career, it's that only death is permanent. Miracles happen. If you'd like, I could make you an appointment with a good urologist in San Antonio. Why, I might even take you there," she added, hoping to lighten the mood, "if you don't mind riding in my flashy car."

"No appointments, Redd. I'll be fine, if you don't make demands I can't meet."

"I won't make demands." Her conscience bopped her upside the head, yet she said, "We could be friends. That's all, simply friends."

"You've always been what's best in ladies."

Blythe smiled, loving the sound of that. Suddenly his aftershave didn't stink. Much.

"If you want to stick around till your reunion," he said, "and if you're interested in something platonic, I'd like that."

It wasn't her reunion—it was theirs. Not that she was wild about attending. *One struggle at a time.*

"You've got a deal."

She heard grass rustle. Eyes opening, she smiled. Tom had flipped to his side and propped up on an elbow to study her.

"Thank you, sweet'eart."

He stroked her cheek, his touch as tender as butterfly wings. His concession made Blythe happy, even special, and his endearment gave her anything but platonic thoughts.

Brushing her ear, he whispered, "True confessions. I've thought about you a million times. The way you used to laugh. And the way you were brave when kids made fun of you. And how you studied to make As. I remember you in the house, working for Granny Myrt. You'd bop around, singing and being silly."

It was nice, hearing his recollections. Warm fuzzies sent her to the verge of tears. "Oh?" was all she allowed herself to utter.

"You had a lot of charm," he admitted. "A mind of your own. Courage. And a strangely different way of looking at the world. Back then, I thought your best features were your eyes and hair, but I've changed my mind. Your best feature is... Think I'll keep you guessing on it."

"Watch out, buddy boy." The warm fuzzies wormed

their way into a cat's curiosity. "You know I can't stand mysteries."

"All right. Your best feature is your red car."

"My what? My— Oh, you! You're teasing me."

He tweaked her nose. "You're fun to tease."

Things were definitely looking up.

The next morning, after Blythe showered in the Saldivars' minuscule bathroom, she borrowed a hair-dryer and started to luxuriate in the electrical appliance. Shelly interrupted her.

The rail-thin girl—the spitting image of her birth mother, Margaret's sister—plopped down on the bathtub's edge. "Talk's all over town," Shelly said. "Everyone knows an ambulance got called last night for Tom Tillman. Is he okay?"

"Just a fainting spell. He checked out fine."

"Whew. That's good to hear." Her brown eyes gleamed. "Mom says you're gonna move out to the Sweet Creek."

"He invited me to stay with him and Myrtle." After he'd tweaked her nose, after E.M.S. left. "I accepted."

"That'll be good for him." She sighed deeply. "I've never forgotten how cool he used to be, when I was little. He was nice to everybody. He doesn't like me much anymore, though."

Blythe studied the eclectically dressed teenager. "It's not that he doesn't like you. He doesn't like much at the moment, including himself. But he's getting there."

Shelly, a tidy girl despite her attire, rearranged bottles on the tub. "Do you think... I asked his granny—would you put in a good word for me? I need a summer job."

"I'm not sure that's a good idea."

"Just my luck. My luck sucks. My boyfriend, well— oh, never mind. I've been everywhere looking for work. Nestor Cantu at Dairy Divine won't even hire me. Says business isn't good enough. I really need a job."

Blythe put things into perspective. Shelly might need pocket money, but the boyfriend part... Evidently the starry-eyed girl had two ambitions. A writing career and wedded bliss. "Your mom says she's worried you'll quit school to get married."

"She thinks marrying young doesn't work. Like with my first mom. Like with Tom and Dana. She says I should wait, like she did. That I won't be happy if I don't get an education and finish my book before, well, you know how it goes. Anyhow, she thinks you and Tom are the only ones who stood a chance as a couple." Shelly eyed her warily. "Y'all gonna get hitched?"

Blythe set the hair-dryer in the cabinet. "No, Shelly. My future isn't in Texas. I'm simply here for the reunion."

"Next thing I know, I'll be at that damn reunion." Forever and always, Tom was dumb. An idiot. Lame-brained as an Irish setter. He still couldn't believe he'd invited Blythe into his home for weeks on end. Last night, when he'd asked, he'd been influenced by bright stars and a beautiful woman.

Yet he wanted her here. He just hoped he could keep his body covered to the neck at all times.

Everything considered, this wasn't a good day. He ached. His starlit trek had him sore to the bone. And it felt as if his skin would burst at the joints. Did he have anything to be thankful for? Yes. Granny Myrt had driven into San Antonio.

Tom ambled into the kitchen; Blythe had thrown open the blinds and made a pitcher of lemonade. "I don't like light," he said. "Shut the blinds. Please."

"Tom, I've seen your face. You're wearing your usual getup. I'm not seeing anything I haven't seen before."

"The dark suits me."

He expected an argument but didn't get it. She drew the blinds together and made her way to the kitchen table, where he parked his used-up self.

"Oops. I forgot the ice." Blythe stirred the pitcher and rearranged a pair of drinking glasses. "Would you get it?"

He wasn't in the habit of fetching. "I don't need ice."

"It's a luxury to me. I don't pass up luxuries."

He frowned, but got a bowl of ice. "Are you happy now?"

"If you like the lemonade as much as I hope you do, I'll be happy." She lobbed a couple of ice cubes into each glass.

He took a sip. "You must be happy. This hits the spot."

A bright smile elbowed its way into her round features. He did favor the way she smiled. She suddenly asked, "What's your opinion of Shelly Saldivar?"

"She's a good kid. I coached her team in softball, when she was nine, then helped her with eighth-grade math. She's mouthy, though."

"That goes with being sixteen."

"Goes with being kin to Margaret."

Blythe opened her lovely mouth; Tom just knew she'd

stick up for her friend. She behaved in character, but twisted his conscience, saying, "If I didn't know you better, I'd think you were criticizing dear Margaret."

"She's a nosy gossip."

"Who sat with Myrtle, day after day, at the hospital. And brought meals here, during your convalescence. And organized a fund-raiser at Fill-Er-Fast to pay the part of your hospital bills your insurance didn't cover— even though you haven't made the teeniest effort to re- pay the community's kindness. You wouldn't do some- thing so mean as to jeer at Margaret."

He squirmed. "Well, I... I, um— Margaret owed me. I gave her money to get set up, when she adopted Shelly." He paused. "You're right. Margaret's okay."

Blythe smiled, victorious. "Tonight I'm going to ask Shelly if she's interested in working for...for me."

"You'd hire her to step-and-fetch-it in my house? Forget it. I don't want people roaming around."

"I'm on holiday. I don't want to be waiting on myself. Or on you. My favorite thing to make for dinner is res- ervations. Make that my *only* thing. I don't cook."

That took him by surprise. As a teenager, he'd pic- tured her in the role of typical wife, at home at her range. So be it. In defense of his stance, he said, "Margaret would fob that dog off on Shelly half the time."

"I like dogs. Like you do. Did. Dogs mean home and hearth and everything cozy." Blythe batted eyelashes to amplify her show of manipulation. "Won't be so bad. You wait and see."

He could argue. He could, but wouldn't. Life, Tom figured, had truly gotten out of his control.

* * *

By later that day Tom made strides in accepting his plight. Being around the redhead didn't prove bad. Blythe made no demands—any *more* demands!—so he ambled onto the front porch. Where were the bamboo shades? No need to ask.

The culprit lounged with sunglasses perched on her cute nose. Reading a magazine titled something on the order of *World Health Journal,* she didn't appear overheated, despite the broiling day. Was she superhuman?

Up to now he hadn't really delved into what she'd done with herself between high school and *World Health Journal.* A widowed nurse who preferred "reservations" could have taken many paths.

A friend should ask after another. He found what little shade he could to sit in a wicker chair. "You know, you haven't told me your proper last name."

The magazine shaded her face. "I'm still Blythe Redd."

"Peculiar. On second thought, the norm would be peculiar with you. If you were my wife, you'd take my name."

"I'm not your wife." She turned a page. "By the way, whatever happened to old Snip?"

"He went to California and took up Zen." Snip's replacement got sent away with Dana Brat.

"Zen, eh? I hear your parents are into that. I hear they've got a split-level house and a swimming pool, and are leading the real California life."

"Dad never was much for ranching." The Sweet Creek once belonged to the maternal side of Tom's family, all long departed. Never a rancher, Tom Senior had itched to fly away. Like his son, he'd had his dreams.

Tom's mother, Evelyn, had helped him realize those dreams. "They do live the California good life."

"Does that bother you?"

"Not at all," Tom answered honestly. "Forget dogs and parents. Where you been all these years?"

Turning another page, she replied in a joking manner, "Teaching aerobics."

"What about the nurse part?"

"Why can't a nurse teach abs and quads?" Lowering the magazine, she grinned impishly. "You know, 'bend in that wheelchair, suck in that gut.'"

"If you teach aerobics, I break broncs."

"You're saying I don't look stair-stepped and butt-flossed?"

"Please."

"Okay, my thighs look like cotton candy." She lifted a glass of lemonade from the nearby table and took a sip. "Name one person who doesn't like cotton candy."

"You look great," he said honestly, eyeing the legs exposed by Bermuda shorts. "You've got fine legs. Big, but muscular and tanned. They look powerful."

"They are. But you're being kind. I have my share of cellulite."

He had the sudden urge to have those legs wrapped around his body. Well, a man could dream, couldn't he? The urge to kiss her became very real. At least he hadn't lost his passion for kisses. *Ease up, Tillman. Don't set yourself up for a fall.*

"All right, Nurse Redd. It's fess-up time. Spill it. Spill it all. What have you been doing with yourself?"

Eyes not meeting his, she set the magazine aside. "I've been... Mostly, I've been in war zones."

"War zones? I thought you'd been married. Or are you one of those women who calls marriage war?"

"When I said 'war zones,' I meant combat. That's where I met my husband, a Frenchman."

It hurt Blythe to discuss her life, Tom could see, but he did have an overactive imagination about her Frenchman. "Go on."

"After Jean-Pierre died…"

Jean-Pierre? Sounds like a real winner. Probably owned a poodle. And wore berets and smocks. Went around kissing everyone's cheek, even the men's.

"After Jean-Pierre died, I joined Partners in Crisis."

Tom swept a hand down his mouth, groaning. It felt as if a cattle prod zapped him. From what he'd heard on the news, he did *not* favor Blythe being tied in with that bunch. They sent medical personnel into the thick of fighting, wherever fighting took place. *Wars are like taxes, they keep on coming.*

"You still with those Partners in Crisis folks?" he asked, dreading her reply.

"I'm on leave. I could be called back any hour, but I've learned not to wait on trouble, else I'd never have the opportunity to enjoy luxuries. I lead a dual life, luxuries and war. They balance out."

This truly was a lousy day. "You could get a job in a regular hospital. Or teach aerobics."

Blythe whipped off her sunglasses, her eyes green sparklers. "I'd never consider that. Partners in Crisis is my life."

"For however long you last."

"For however long I last."

"I don't like it. I don't like it a damn bit."

Those green eyes went cool. "It's not your call, Tom."

"Okay, I don't have rights over you." None but a friend's right. Any good friend would caution another. "Didn't your Frenchman object when you traipsed into battle?"

"Of course he didn't."

"Marriage means—well, the men I know expect certain things out of their wives, which means being a wife, not running all over the globe, picking up body parts and dodging bullets."

"My, my. Aren't we the provincial?" she said snidely.

He did a slow burn. "Call me a dumb cowboy. *Ex*-cowboy. Stuck in the wilds, assuming all marriages work the American way."

"Margaret told me you and Dana fought like dogs. Is that your idea of the American way?"

"That Saldivar woman ought to register her mouth with the National Park Service."

"If you're ever in the market for a wife again, you'd do well to study Jean-Pierre's style of husbanding. *Très magnifique.*"

"If he was so hot, why didn't you take his name?"

She let loose with a string of French-sounding words, probably the equivalent of "Kiss my grits."

"You've become some sort of goofball European," Tom charged.

She blistered him with a look that baked like the sun. "I'll have you know, I'm still a citizen. I pay taxes and own my condo. When I'm on leave, I'm usually in Delray Beach. And I don't appreciate your belittling Europeans. Continental men are the world's most gallant.''

"That settles it.'' He shot from his chair, stomped to her. Before he could remember that leveling dares took strength, he bore down. His hands gripped the arms of her chair, when he wanted to grip Blythe. "You want gallant, pussycat?''

"You haven't called me 'pussycat' in a long time.''

"I should've kept you here with me.'' He scooted a wedge between her knees and knelt toward her face. "If you hadn't left, you wouldn't have harebrained ideas.''

"Name one thing you did to keep me.''

"You were seventeen. Your father had control over you.''

"You could have asked his permission.''

"Yeah. I should have. I didn't. So sue me.''

Impulse got the better of Tom. One hand left the chair's arm. It found a plump hip, then Blythe's waist. Despite his aches and pains, he found the strength to gather her to him.

"I'm going to kiss you,'' he promised, ignoring better judgment. "I'm going to give you a good ol' Texas version of an American kiss.''

"I thought we were going to keep this on a friendly basis.''

"Call it anything you please.'' His mouth swooped to hers. Lemonade oil tasted tart on her lips. She had a sharp edge to her, anyhow. He enjoyed things on the tart side.

He felt something stir in a long-dead place. Strange. Weird. Was this happening? Must have been something he ate. Before he could analyze it any further, Blythe pushed him away.

This was worse than battle. Blythe sank onto her borrowed bed in the spare room, wondering what the dickens she'd gotten into. Being with Tom could be hazardous to mental health.

"I need my head examined," she muttered under her breath. "This thing with Tom is driving me up the wall."

In school he'd been open-minded, full of dreams. And she'd loved him for it. But now the last thing she needed was involvement, even platonic, with some irascible close-minded cowboy who'd cramp her style. Besides, she didn't like it when he'd goaded her about Jean-Pierre. It wasn't something she liked to think about, her husband dying.

As for Tom, their yesterdays and today weren't the same, with one big exception. His lips tasted as good as ever.

"I should've listened to a different Tom. Tom Wolfe was right. You can't go home again."

"Talking to me?" Her Tom strolled into her bedroom.

"I'm not. Furthermore, this visiting arrangement isn't a good idea. I'm going to rent a room at the Scott Motel." Better yet, she could head out IH-10, straight for the Atlantic.

"The Scott has bedbugs," Tom informed her.

"So does this place. *You.*"

"I'm not that bad." Tom sat next to her on the bed. He took her hand. Softly. "I shouldn't have passed judgment on your life-style. We shouldn't have kissed. Forgive me?''

"It's not the kiss I regret. I like your kisses. You were always good at them. But I'm not here to muddle my head. Your head. Our heads.''

"We went haywire, when you first arrived at my porch.''

"We're not prepared for the intensity of each other.''

They looked into each other's eyes. Blythe saw sadness in Tom's. She knew her own heart. It was a mess.

"Yoo-hoo! Where y'all at?''

"Myrtle,'' Blythe said.

At the same moment, Tom muttered, "Granny Myrt.''

Before either could alight from bed, Myrtle swept in, her fingers filled with strings holding a balloon bouquet. Her lined face in fuller bloom than the balloons, Myrtle tripped over to her grandson and houseguest. "I'm happy as a pig in wallow! Looky here. My favorite people, abed together!''

"We were sitting on the edge of it,'' Blythe tried to explain. "That's all.''

"Sitting leads to resting, which leads to—''

"Granny Myrt—''

"Don't say a thing. Don't say nothing else!'' She danced a double step. "I'm tickled to death. You two back together, where you always belonged. Why, it won't be any time till I'm free to do my own thing.''

Both Blythe and Tom gawked at Myrtle, then at each other.

"I'm gonna end up in Hollywood, that's what I'm gonna do. I'll study Zen. I'll buy me a travel trailer. And a red convertible!'' Myrtle thrust balloon strings at

Blythe. "I'm gonna get me one of them jobs in TV, yes, I am. They hire old ladies. TV commercials. I'm gonna be famous!"

Blythe groaned. How did Myrtle expect to break into the big time, when she couldn't read a script? Poor woman. Poor delusional Myrtle. Middle-age crazies at age seventy-four.

Who needed these complications? Florida sounded better and better to Blythe. Actually, her beeper had gone off this morning, Partners in Crisis's managing director having called to mention a symposium in Miami on trauma care.

"Redd won't be staying," Tom said with purpose.

"Honey girl?"

"He's right."

"Oh, no." White curls shook with disappointment.

"You're unhappy here, Granny Myrt? That's sad. I'm hurt. But why should a grandson like me hold you back? If you want to strike out for Hollywood, I won't keep you. Don't worry. I'll get by." He sighed heavily, the rat. "Somehow."

His ploy worked. Myrtle's face fell. "I shouldn't have…I didn't mean to…" The shine left her eyes. "I thought y'all was making up for lost time. I'll go start supper."

"I've got a hankering for steak and scalloped potatoes," Tom announced.

Blythe could have bopped him.

"Steak and potatoes." Myrtle took the balloons from Blythe and trudged away.

Tom left, too. For several seconds Blythe stayed put, then anger roused her to act. She sped to the kitchen where Myrtle stood at the counter, slicing potatoes, the balloons nowhere in sight. "Myrtle, put down that paring knife."

It fell. "What?"

"Give me your best imitation of Liz Taylor. That's good. Now Katharine Hepburn. You need to work on that. How about the lady who sells Church's chicken? Excellent!"

"Honey girl, I ain't going to La La Land. I'm gonna stay right here, where I belong."

"You raised your son, and saw after Tom. You did what was expected of you. And more. It's time for *Myrtle*."

"It's time for supper," her grandson bellowed from across the kitchen.

Blythe glared at his wild blond hair, especially at his hard eyes. "They're holding a cell for you at the nuthouse on South Presa," she said through clenched teeth. "You belong there."

He had the audacity to laugh.

After he'd made an exit, Myrtle turned to Blythe. "It's no wonder you don't want him. He's sure not the boy I raised, or you loved." Tears sprang. "He used to be good and kind. Everybody depended on my Tom. And he never hurt nobody."

"I think down deep he's the same old Tom," Blythe surmised aloud, doubting her words as she said them, but willing to say anything to make her elderly friend feel better.

Myrtle sniffed. "His inviting you here means something. If you'd get him back around folks, I suspect that'd help."

"Don't you worry. For starters, I'll hire Shelly Saldivar for housework, so you'll be freed up. And Tom's going to attend our reunion. I think once the ice is broken, he'll be himself again. It's going to take some doing, but *my* will be done."

Myrtle grinned.

Blythe surged from the kitchen to find Tom in the living room, watching a rerun of "I Love Lucy." "You're dandruff, you're soap scum, you're toe jam," she stormed, not about to give any quarter. "You ought to be fried up like potatoes."

"Come again?"

Fried. Where was her head? Mortified at her callous remark, she started to try to smooth her blunder. *Forget it.* "I'm going to send Myrtle to town to one of those crash-learning centers. She *is* going to read."

Wordlessly, he punched the channel changer, surfing to a shopping station.

Realizing the magnitude of living up to her oaths, yet unable to stuff a mental sock in her big mouth, Blythe announced, "I'll do my best to help when she's ready to storm Hollywood."

"Old ladies need to be settled, not cavorting around."

"Good thing no one ever said that to Mother Teresa. Or Georgia O'Keefe. Or—"

"Where does Ma Barker come in?"

A hawker on TV began to sell youth cream; Blythe grabbed the control and threw it to a far corner. "Sit there like a chunk of beef. See if I care! But stand informed. I do have connections in Hollywood, and I'll use them for Myrtle."

"You what?" His mouth dropped.

"I'm in thick with a big-shot director, Oliver Rockford," Blythe overemphasized. She'd met the egomaniac when he'd made a war movie in Afghanistan—they had eaten at the same dive. He probably no more remembered her than he did the kid who'd hauled water on the movie set.

"You read Rockford's name on a marquee," Tom said with a curdling scowl. "That's all."

"You wait and see."

"Seeing's believing."

Yeah, well, he might have her on that. But she'd take one step at a time. She huffed over to the telephone, thumbed through the directory, then got Dairy Divine on the line. "Nestor?" On the off chance that Margaret's daughter might have stopped at the drive-in, Blythe took a gamble. "Is Shelly Saldivar there? Good. Send her to Sweet Creek Ranch with three steak-finger baskets— make it four if she hasn't eaten. Add an extra pint of gravy to it."

Tom kicked his heel against the recliner's hassock. "You'll clog our arteries with fat! Some nurse you are."

"Send Tom Tillman the check," she said to Nestor.

She set the phone in its cradle.

Tom glared. "I thought you were leaving."

She started to shout, "That's what you get for thinking," but stopped short. She'd stumbled on an iota of sagacity. "I'm a hypocrite," she confessed. "I don't want you to change me, yet I'm determined to change you. We don't tolerate well."

A smile—the smile of Terrific Tom—spilled over angular features to settle in the clear blue of his eyes. He winked and crooked a finger. "Come on over here, sweet'eart. Come over and sit down next to this dumb ol' beat-up cowboy. Please.''

Her fizzle fizzed, she went to him. Knelt next to the recliner with her head on his arm. A tender yet strong hand stroked her head, his fingers combing her hair. She felt his energy connect with hers. Was there a better, more reassuring feeling in the world, than the comfort of a touch?

"You rat. Every time you get me to the point of crying uncle, you say or do something to turn it around.''

"What's new there?" Tom spoke quietly, yet with a timbre of openness and promise. "Blythe Redd, looks like we've both got a lot to learn, or at least to study on. Looks like we've got a spell of time to do it. We could give it a shot.''

Goodbye, Miami symposium.

Chapter Four

It didn't take long, inasmuch as Blythe didn't tarry with anything, for Tom to realize how quickly one woman could finish upending routine.

By noon of the day following their argument over Hollywood and its ilk, her hired girl had reported for work. Blythe had also driven Granny Myrt into San Antonio, enrolled her in Readers Center and returned alone to the ranch—if he were to discount her package-laden arms or the delivery van that followed her up the driveway.

While a pair of burly workers put wrenches and screwdrivers to her big purchase in the kitchen, she set Shelly Saldivar to raising shades and washing parlor windows.

That wasn't all.

"What is this?" Ignoring the now-assembled delivery—a steel contraption that looked like one of those steel-horse fitness monsters one could order on TV for fifty a month, for a zillion months—Tom started to sweep a hand to indicate the bottles and gadgets that Blythe arranged on the kitchen table.

Nippy jumped to a chair, distracting him. "Get down, dog!"

Just as Tom feared would happen, Shelly had indeed brought the dog with her.

Looking crisp as starch in a cotton blouse and capri pants and smelling fine in her exotic perfume, Blythe scooped the Pomeranian up and pointed him toward the dining area, its sole purpose having been reduced to storage for boxes of medical receipts and legal papers, plus income-tax archival.

Once Nippy's nails had tip-tapped out of hearing range, Blythe motioned to gadgetry, potions and a case of diet supplement drink. "I've decided to put you on a get-fit program. You'll need your strength, so snack on the Ensuromedic. I'm going to start you with three minutes a day on the exerciser. Don't worry. You'll limber up from massages. How're you doing with the rubber ball?"

"Don't be spending big money on me. Little money, either."

She got one of those aggravating sunny smiles. "Myrtle loaned me your credit card to buy everything."

"First my privacy, then my home. Now my wallet. Is nothing sacred to you?" He legged it over to the thief, who looked infinitely pleased with herself. "I'm assuming you forged my signature."

"I did." A confident nod of soft curls followed. "By

the way, I've hired a Swedish fellow from San Antonio to be your masseur. He agreed to accept your credit card.''

"Not on your life. No man's going to put his hands on me. Forget it.'' Tom rushed onward, "If you want me massaged, *you'll* have to do it.''

"Well, if you insist.''

From her expression, Tom realized there had never been a masseur. He'd been set up. Adrenaline seeped, replaced by trepidation. Once, when he and Dana made a trip to Las Vegas, he had indulged in a massage at the hotel's spa. Nudity beneath a thin white sheet with bright lights above hadn't been a problem, but at a time like this, all bets were off.

"The masseur was planning to bring his own table, so we'll have to make do. I think—'' Cocking a hip, Blythe sloped toward the table to pat it once. "This will do. It's sturdy.''

"Got it all planned out, do you? What if I say no?'' Tom crept toward the bold redhead.

"You mentioned a 'spell of time' to 'study on' what needs to be done. Should I take it you're not good at your word?''

"My word is good. Mostly.''

The tip of her chin crept upward. "Prove it.''

Judicious thought escaped him, as it had since her return. Blame it on the scent of this woman. Blame it on the sight of her. Blame it on her aggravating, wholly intriguing presence. A sudden, certain urge took charge, the impulse to kiss the lips now parted a fraction of an inch, challenging him.

Give it up, Tillman. Peace won't come from kisses.

They'll lead to expectations you're not capable of meeting.

His voice lowering an octave, he asked, "Redd, are you going to leave me any dignity whatsoever?"

"Stripping your dignity is the last thing I want." Her voice had lowered, too. To the sweetest part of her range. "I want to give you dignity. I want..." Eyes sparkling, she lifted her palm to place it on his chest. "What I really want is for you to kiss me."

He almost did. His willpower ranked right up there with his strength of limb and libido. Lousy. Warmth rushed through his veins in a reminder of what it felt like to be whole and needy and accepting of a gift much better than pitching a no-hitter.

That warmth didn't quite reach where it ought to, though.

Tempted to trace a forefinger along her bottom lip, forcing his fingers not to move, he managed to say, "Would Florence Nightingale seduce a patient into doing her bidding?"

"In the Crimean War she did engage in what we now call sex therapy. Or so the rumor goes."

"Is that so?" he teased. "Done much sex therapy yourself?"

"None." Blythe blushed. A good old-fashioned blush, like when he used to rag her about having such beautiful breasts.

I bet they're still beautiful.

"Be ready for the massage at five o'clock," she demanded. "I've got to pick Myrtle up at six-thirty. Starting tomorrow, she'll drive herself. I must stop at a restaurant on the way home, for take-out. We're having chef salads for dinner."

He heard every word she said, but "five o'clock" stuck. "That's not much time for me to get used to the massage idea."

"Time waits for neither man nor beast, if I might borrow an axiom." She rearranged the stockpile on the table, her fingers working swiftly and efficiently. "I won't be here forever. We're talking time management, Tom. And practicality."

He tore his gaze from the cleavage revealed by her bending to her chore. Sex therapy obviously didn't appeal to her. So be it. But why? Why did he get that old familiar feeling? Or did he?

Nerves had him gripped, he figured.

She'd returned on a pity mission. She had a life. He had none. This pity mission would end, and she'd go back to bullets and bandages—the hardest to accept being the last part. Even though he hadn't a clue about what the future might hold, Tom mumbled, "Practical."

"Solid planning makes for success."

Making her way to the back porch, she hummed a tune. The march from that old Alec Guinness war movie about a bridge.

"Practical," Tom murmured again as the screen door slammed shut. He anchored a shoulder against a doorjamb, needing strength in more ways than he wished to study.

A pillar of practical strength described Redd, though. How would she have taken it, had she been the one burned?

What drove her to a sadistic streak?

At that moment Nippy padded into the kitchen again. The Pomeranian had a truculent look in his round black eyes, as one of Tom's house shoes dangled from his furred jaw. "Grrrrr" worked its way around leather.

"*Et tu,* Nippy?" Tom rubbed the side of his nose. "Must I be challenged by everyone and everything in my own household?"

Nippy repositioned the shoe, as a cigar aficionado might roll a stogie to the other side of his mouth, not giving it up, not giving an inch. Inexorable beneath a No Smoking sign.

"Listen up, boyo. If we're going to do the home-and-hearth bit, we've got to get the rules right. The dog fetches the slipper, not eats it."

Nippy backed toward the dining room.

"Give it up, little fellow. I'm the boss here." Maybe. Tom bent down as much as he could. "Come here. Let's you and me have a chat, mano-a-mano."

Nippy ran off with his prize as well as the battle.

"Drop it," Tom heard Shelly demand from the living room.

Shaking his head, Tom got a Big Red from the fridge. Redd's midnight raid of the past evening had left a sizable void in the interior, with the exception of beer and Ensuromedic. The woman did like to eat. He liked to watch her eat. She had zest. He admired zest.

Before he could take the soda pop to his room, the harsh lights of the parlor being too much to deal with, Shelly pranced into the kitchen, wearing cutoffs and a T-shirt. The word "big" in all caps covered her chest. Her coarse black hair looked as if it had been spar-varnished to make it stand on end. And her bust was not big.

She lifted the retrieved house slipper level with her sparse chest. "He didn't hurt it," she said. "Nippy's kinda neurotic. He can't help it. He's just that way. Whenever Mom's not around, he chews stuff. I hope you won't be mad at him."

Tom shrugged. "I'm getting used to things that're beyond my control."

"Can I have one of those Big Reds?"

"Make yourself at home," he said, uncertain how honest the offer had been. Whatever the case, he knew he'd better get inured to her presence. "The fridge is open to you, anytime."

"Thanks. My mom doesn't let me have but one soda a day. Says they're too expensive to be wasted. And bad for my teeth. Mom's got a thing about teeth." Shelly smoothed the side of her hideous hair, then strolled over to the refrigerator and ducked her head inside. "Tom…you mind if I ask a question?"

Yes, he minded. Chatting with the teenager ranked in allure with bearing his scars to bright lights and nosy fingers. *Don't be rough on her.* She'd been a good kid, eager to learn. And he did feel bad about not hiring her earlier. The Saldivars mostly lived on love. Which didn't buy school clothes or hair shellac.

"Go ahead," he allowed. "Ask away."

The girl tripped over to the kitchen table to take a chair. "Aren't you gonna sit down?"

He did. "What's up, Shelly?"

"I have a boyfriend. You know him. Icky Kuleska."

Tom hadn't seen the kid lately, but from what he remembered, he thought Shelly, even with her Olive Oyl build and unfortunate hair, could do better. "I know him."

"I love Icky. But I wonder sometimes if he loves me. Now that he's graduated, he's got plans, and this cow-patty burg cramps his style. There's not much to do around here, you know, unless you drive into San Antonio. Which isn't saying much. That town is tacos and the family channel," she said, ignoring the Alamo and other attractions, and adding the frown of a teenager bored with the familiar. "It's no place for a dude who's gonna be a rap star."

What? Tom couldn't picture the pasty-faced dolt having a lick of stage presence. "Rap star?"

"He's got the jive for it."

Tom didn't know much about the rap scene, but he sensed danger. "Stay away from him."

Shelly ignored the warning. "Once he leaves, I'm afraid he'll forget me, like you did Blythe."

"What makes you think I forgot Blythe?"

"You married straight off after she left—my mom said so. Maybe I should keep my mouth shut, but..." Shelly took a long pull from the aluminum can, then settled it against her cheek, apparently to cool the fresh rise of blood. "I have a hard time keeping my mouth shut."

"Don't torture yourself, Shelly," Tom said dryly. "Some things can't be bred out of a family."

"Well, okay. About Blythe... She's kinda pretty."

"Not kind of. She is pretty."

"Don't think I'm criticizing her, I'm not. She's nice, even if she is, well—the way I see it, you obviously weren't all that crazy about her, her being fat and all. The other boys did tease you."

"That was their problem, not mine, if they couldn't appreciate her beauty. And you got it wrong, Shelly." Frankly, Tom couldn't believe he defended past actions. Time did change everything. "You're mistaken about me and Redd."

"Well, why didn't you marry her or something?"

Tom rubbed his suddenly aching neck. "You ask questions that're too personal."

"My mom says you two could've made a great team."

That woman's mouth must have been Ground Zero when the asteroid struck and sent dinosaurs into extinction.

Of course, Tom could make dinosaur tracks to leave. Strangely, he found himself saying, "Margaret's right. We would've been great together, forever. But we were kids, Shelly. Too young to be married." He'd learned fast on that score. "I had college ahead of me, and dreams that—"

"Mom says you never got to college. She says you were going just to get some talent scout to notice you, so you could say goodbye to tacos and cowpatties. I've heard about your dreams. You wanted to be a Major League pitcher. Yankee Stadium is what you were after."

It was Tom's turn for his face to heat. "Like you said, this burg doesn't have much going for it."

"Half the boys I know want to be sports stars. It's like me thinking I'll become Miss America. You probably wouldn't have made it."

Out of the mouths of babes! Icky Kuleska ought to listen to his babe.

Jiving Icky not being Tom Tillman's business, he centered on that which was. "Redd would have stood by my side while I tried." Unlike Dana the brat. "If I'd failed, we could have come back to Sweet Creek. To raise cattle and rear kids."

"I dunno." Shelly poked a fingertip into her hair; the whole of it moved as she scratched her head. "I can't see it, Blythe a housewife. She's like somebody you read about. Miss America with a mission. Going off to Europe, being a war nurse, marrying some dude who looked like that movie star, Louis Jourdan. I saw a photo of her main squeeze. I asked to see one. She had a snapshot. Yummy, for an old dude."

"Old dude?" Had Monsieur Beret died of old age?

"You know. Middle-aged. Probably about forty."

Tom groaned at her youthful image of hung-up-to-dry. He personally felt ancient short of thirty-five, but what of it? He kept thinking about Blythe. He drew a mental image of her, dashing here and there, living a life as glamorous as anyone in China Grove could ever conjure up. Chunks from war movies next flashed before his eyes, not a glamorous vision.

"My mom says Blythe fulfilled her destiny," Shelly stated.

"Your mother ought to apply for Dear Abby's job."

"She is pretty smart, my mom." Shelly grinned, showing nice teeth. "Did you know I like to write? I won the school essay contest last year. I want to write books. Biographies. I'm gonna write about Blythe and her adventures."

"Redd's too young for a biography. She's not through living her life."

"My mom thinks it's time she settled down and married you. I don't see it. You're just Tom. The old dude who's a hermit, out here on a ranch that doesn't even have any cattle or horses. Makes for a dull ending."

At least Shelly hadn't mentioned his injuries. What luck. Damn. *I'm starting to think like Redd, finding the good apple among the rotten ones.* "Don't you have work to do?"

"Uh-huh. I do." Shelly stood and lobbed her empty Big Red into the trash. "I never did get around to asking you this one thing about Icky, though."

"Why don't you ask your mother?"

Tom had already headed toward his room, where Nippy had destroyed the mate to the house slipper, leaving masticated leather in the middle of his double bed.

"Dog," he muttered as if the Pomeranian had stuck around to gloat. "Much more, and I'll make a neck pillow out of your hide."

Tom shoved the house shoe to the floor and plopped down. The mattress at his spine, a forearm shielding his eyes, he fell to serious thinking. Shelly had been right. Blythe was the stuff of printed words.

He, on the other hand, was no Louis Jourdan, no Jean-Pierre. Never had been, never would be. He was Tom. Just plain Tom. Single syllable. A plain name, a beat-up wretch who used to be a man. One hombre of no particular achievement. Born on a simple scrap of South Texas dirt. Born here, existed here, and would die here, probably in the same iron bed where he'd laid his head for each of his thirty-three years. To be buried in the churchyard not two miles from this house, his tombstone inscription shortened to Returned Unopened.

Tired and weary, he closed his eyes. And awoke to the words, "Tom! It's time for your massage."

Not five minutes into the massage, Blythe grew exasperated. "Tom, you've got to let me lower this sheet. You'll get more benefit if my hands make contact."

He nuzzled into the layers of blankets that padded the table, his voice muffled as he said, "It feels okay, the way you're doing it."

Patience. Once he lets you see him the first time, you can get past this fear of his. Already she'd closed the kitchen shades, dimming natural light to save his dignity. A wholesale inspection? Not unless he was ready for it. Which he wasn't.

Nor was he ready for kisses. It still embarrassed Blythe, how he'd refused to kiss her. Not only today, but ever since she'd moved in. Well, except for that one kiss that she'd aggravated him into. Might be a lesson in his reticence.

What he needed was to relax.

And she needed to decide just how far she'd go with his therapy, which might end up the Nightingale method. She believed his impotency was psychosomatic. Curable.

As well, she found him very attractive, scars and all, but did he want *Blythe Redd* to cure him? He probably didn't know what he wanted.

If someone had pinned her down, she doubted if she could give a lucid answer, either.

She bent to reacquaint—no! run—her fingers through

the thick strands of his unbound hair. He'd left off with the Bulgarian bath. The pure scent of man and shampoo wafted. This appealed to her.

"How about if I just put my hand under this sheet and scratch your back?" she murmured. "You remember when you used to scratch my back?"

His head reared up; she detected the smallest of smiles. "I remember. We'd sit on the porch steps, evening times. I'd end up on the top step, you sitting between my knees. I swear, you purred like a pussycat."

A smile tugged her lips, too. She poured health-store massage oil into the cup of her palm. "Let me make you purr, tomcat."

Her fingers slid beneath the sheet to his wide shoulders. He still had muscles—not a lot, but they were there. As in the past, he felt good to her. It was all she could do not to think too much about times gone by.

Eyes closed, she let her kneading, stroking fingers assess his back. If he had scars, there weren't many. He hadn't been hurt running *from* anything.

Too bad his courage had deserted him.

When her hands touched his ribs, beneath his armpits, though, the texture of his skin changed. It was dried, ridged. Scar tissue. She felt him tense beneath her touch.

"Relax," she whispered. He made an effort.

Covertly as possible she extracted her fingers to pour more oil into her palm. Pull the sheet down, just an inch or two, she told herself. Nothing drastic, simply where she could rub the oil in, then go for more without losing the flow of movement.

The moment she tugged the sheet's hem down, though, Tom reacted.

"That's enough with the massage," he snapped.

Her fingers opened. The linen dropped. "Okay. No problem." There was a problem, of course. She wondered at her own lack of patience. Or did it mostly have to do with the invisible barrier between them?

She compelled a smile. "Take a nice long soak, while I go to town for Myrtle. Use some of that bath oil—it's in the green bottle. It's great for the skin. It'll help you relax, enjoy your chef's salad and get a good night's sleep."

He would need his rest. Tomorrow she'd make certain he started getting back in the saddle.

Sunglasses magically appeared at breakfast, beside Tom's fork. He slipped them on. They did filter sunlight, which was a help, because the moment the last bite of biscuit slid down his gullet, Blythe demanded his exercise sessions commence on the porch.

Dragging the steel monster outside, Blythe pulling while he pushed, Tom struggled. By the time he mounted the saddle and Nurse Redd began ratcheting out instructions, he'd come up with a new name for her. "Generalissima." Dictator.

It didn't take long for another name to come to mind, this one for the steel bronc. It wasn't Old Paint. He chose Diablo.

Devil.

Tom strained. He huffed, puffed. He was sweating. Out of breath. The sunglasses slipped, threatened to fly off.

"Keep it up. Don't stop. We must raise our cardios," Blythe encouraged.

"We? You got a...mouse in...your shorts pocket?"

Ignoring his remark, and sorting through flats of flower seedlings and hanging pots—she probably planned to do the gardening bit between orders—Generalissima Blythe continued to hector about pace and heart rates, until he wanted to threaten her life. He would have if he'd had the energy.

"Enough," he said between gasps of breath.

"You've only been riding it for—" she glanced at her wristwatch "—ninety seconds."

Tom quit Diablo. "I've had it. 'Nuff said."

"Don't stop now. You'll lose the aerobic benefit. You need to make three minutes, then gradually build up to twenty. You can pretty much be there by the reunion."

The reunion? Never.

"It's hot out here." He adjusted the sunglasses. "Why can't I ride this thing in the air-conditioned parlor, where I can watch Oprah?"

"Perspiration cleans the pores, rids the body of toxins."

He wiped his brow and beneath the shades. "You take a turn then. You could probably use some exercise, too."

"I do. Get going again on the rider, Tom. I'll follow my own program while you do yours."

Grudgingly, he spurred Diablo. And got a shock when Blythe vaulted over the porch railing, then scaled it handily.

He went inert. "What...in hell's name...are you doing?"

"Climbing the rail." Once more she jumped up and over, then sprang to the ground. Again she hiked her heel onto the porch lip and swung up and over. Such labor didn't even break the cadence of her voice, as she explained, "I climb for exercise. Mountains, molehills. Whatever's handy. Makes no difference."

It went without asking why such exertion didn't pare down her silhouette: the midnight fridge raids of Redd Revere.

"Why?" he asked solemnly.

"You ever climb a cable or a rope ladder to a hovering helicopter?" Still she rose hand over hand with remarkable grace. Her face didn't even flush.

He gave Diablo another feeble kick in the flanks. "Trying to embarrass me? No, I haven't climbed into helicopters."

"You do need fitness for it. Cables are a bitch, but ladders can be fun, if guns aren't firing at your behind."

"Sounds too military for me."

She paused for a moment and swept an errant curl from her forehead. "Well, you could always scramble into a boat in rough seas. That's pretty much a kick, too. And not as strenuous as helicopters. Ever done any deep-sea diving?"

"No."

"Snorkeling?"

"No."

"I understand the snorkeling is pretty good in San Marcos. No rough seas. Just a nice clear river." Another dive over the railing. "We could drive up there. You could give it a try."

"Why is it every one of our conversations disintegrate into how you plan to torture my body?"

"Not every conversation."

He elevated a fist to strangle air. "Would you stop that damn climbing!"

"I wouldn't dream of it. Not till I've done at least twenty minutes."

Tom could take no more of her superhuman display. He struggled off Diablo and scuttled indoors. He might as well have mounted a swaying ladder, so rough did he find the haul to the fridge for a cold one—a beer, even if five o'clock wouldn't come for hours.

Somehow, he finally achieved the recliner.

Big sigh.

Peace.

Peace didn't last too long. Blythe popped in the door. She hadn't broken a sweat, although her cheeks bore the healthy glow of exercise. Grounds for justifiable homicide, he decided.

With the sweetness usually found tucked into little pink packets, she asked, "Are you giving up?"

"Yes."

She walked over and took the last swallow of his beer. "Yum. But you'd get more nutrition from Ensuromedic."

"I'm going to strangle you. As soon as I rest up."

Lashes fluttered. Her smile aggravated him even more. She said, "I don't suppose there's a chance you'd help me plant those impatiens?"

"Do you realize you live under a death wish?"

"So, Tom... what's it like, living like you're dead?" Turning on her heel, Blythe marched across the rug. "Quitter."

Marching to the porch, Blythe attacked the impatiens with a vengeance. She repotted them, before using excess energy and anger to collect tools to hang the airplane plants. Drat him. Drat that sourpuss, Mr. Unterrific.

Why couldn't he be tough, like Jean-Pierre?

"That's unfair," she muttered.

Jean-Pierre had gone unscathed, till the end. He'd broken when she'd been wounded in Sarajevo. When he'd visited the cot where she'd laid, gut-shot and burning with fever, Jean-Pierre had cried. Her big strong husband had cried.

"I understand why you feel as if you must stay with the organization," he had said, holding her hand. "You can give your love *sans souci,* and know you'll never have your heart broken. It may stop your heart. But if you are taken, you'll die at peace with yourself."

Too weak to speak, she'd silently vowed to make up for not giving the whole of her love to him. Before that moment she'd always held back a corner of her heart, in fear that if she gave too much, Jean-Pierre would hurt her, as Tom had.

She didn't get the chance to embrace her husband with her all. He'd stepped on a land mine that very night and had died before dawn...without his wife to hold his hand.

For Blythe, quitting had been impossible, especially after losing Jean-Pierre. Nursing in war zones was what she did. "It's what I am."

She now plugged an electric drill into a socket, muttered every curse word she'd ever heard in any language, and brushed tears away. "Poor Jean-Pierre. I preferred a quitter to him."

* * *

Quitter. Blythe's charge hurt. Tom wasn't a quitter. Was he? Once Oprah finished for the day, he clutched the remote control and studied the rubber ball. Should he...

At that moment Shelly waltzed from the bedroom hallway.

"Shelly, you ever been to the river at San Marcos?"

"It's loads of fun. Sun, water, picnics. You can explore the caves, or go see Ralph the Swimming Pig at the Springs."

Outdoor fun meant short-sleeved shirts and swim-trunks. Those days were over for him. But it would be nice to get in shape enough to do something, somewhere.

Ignoring the rubber ball, he went to the window. Blythe was drilling holes in the porch ceiling to hang her airplane plants. Did she never wear out?

He moved his gaze to Diablo. What would it hurt to give that steel stallion an honest try? Best not with Generalissima around. He'd break that bronc while she ran errands. Maybe he'd surprise her in a few days' time, by showing her Tom Tillman wasn't such a hopeless case. In the meantime Blythe Redd could suffer, thinking her plans didn't work.

"Would serve that dictator right."

Might serve her right, true, but Tom realized how good Blythe was for him. That was the *right* in all of this.

Chapter Five

Ice cream. That was what Blythe wanted, a big dish of it. A huge dish of it. Ice cream would make her feel better. Medicine for the psyche. "Make it chocolate."

Sitting in a booth at Dairy Divine—a place pungent with greasy hamburgers, tacos and fries, as well as the clog of cigarette smoke—she eased a glance at the quartet of geezers who occupied a table for four.

Their searching gazes and snippets of conversation bespoke curiosity over the lady stranger in their midst. Perhaps some remembered her—she wouldn't ask. Their teeth sank into the house specialities when the men weren't gossiping, sipping coffee or dragging on those cigarettes.

Death by indulgence, she thought. Almost as good as sex. There wasn't much else in China Grove to do, save for oral gratification. *Go for it, guys. I intend to, too.*

She dipped a spoon into the large mound of chocolate ice cream.

"You plannin' on filling up afore supper?"

Myrtle. Somehow Blythe had missed her entrance to the café. "This is dinner. I won't be at the ranch tonight to eat."

"I thought you favored them swanky restaurants."

"I do, but I've got to go with the flow." Before Myrtle launched into questions, Blythe asked, "How was school?"

"I've got those *ABC*s down, I sure do. Wanna hear them?"

"Go for it."

Myrtle sang the *ABC* song. Finished, she said, "I'm learning Dick and Jane, too. My instructor says when I get good enough, I can move on to romance novels. I always wanted to read 'em. Margaret says they're real good."

"I should say so. I have racks of them at my condo." Blythe reached to pat her hand. "I'm proud of you, Myrtle."

Nestor Cantu approached, wiping his fingers on a towel. "You want anything, Miz Tillman?"

"Gimme one of them ice creams. Make it strawberry. I worked me up an appetite. Won't spoil my dinner, for sure. I've got me a healthy appetite, just like my honey girl here."

Once Nestor delivered her order and returned to the grill, Myrtle frowned. "What's wrong with you?"

"Ennui."

After getting a definition of the strange word, Myrtle asked, "Tom being contrary?"

Inert better fit him. "He's…I don't know—distant?"

"You didn't like that hair-trimming I give him?"

Setting down the spoon that perched halfway to her mouth, Blythe thought about the new look. While still longer than she was accustomed to, Tom's golden hair at least looked neat and orderly, clubbed or not. "His hair looks good."

"He's been slatherin' on Balkan Breeze, too."

Ugh. Actually, she'd poured the bottle down the toilet just this afternoon. "Balkan Breeze isn't the problem." Not anymore.

"Then what's the problem, honey girl?"

"It's not him. Not entirely. It's me." It hadn't been his fault that she'd overrated his abilities and deeds. As for moping over Jean-Pierre, she'd done her grieving for two years, and knew he wouldn't approve of more. "I'm having trouble adjusting to China Grove."

Blythe recalled the pair of teenage girls who'd been ordering tacos when she'd walked in. They had whispered and pointed, reminding Blythe of butt-of-joke years. While she'd gone a long way in changing the way she looked at herself, ridicule still hurt.

"One can plant only so many…flowers." She ate another spoonful of the timeless anti-inflammatory to medicate ridicule.

She dreaded the reunion. All those local yokels, sizing her up and calling names. Dumb as that body wrap had been her demand for Tom to attend it with her. Anyway, what was to say he'd go?

"I get tired of busywork. I don't know what to do. I've got to do something." *It's too late to sign up for the Miami symposium.* "It goes without saying, I'm not into cooking. The only dish I can prepare is Lilith's asparagus soup. She's a nurse I know. The staff at her hospital put together a cookbook. Anyway, Jean-Pierre loved asparagus, so—''

"Tom don't like asparagus."

"Think I'll drive into San Antonio to a bookstore."

"Tom's got a bunch of books in his room. You could borrow some. I've got a better idea. I'll make myself scarce tonight. There's some homemade chicken enchiladas in the freezer. They're dang good. Got some candles left over from Christmas. Look in the cupboard, next to my vitamin E." Myrtle put down her spoon. "Why don't you stop in the liquor store? Get a nice bottle of somethin' smooth. You and Tom make a night of it."

"That's not a good idea, candles and booze."

"Why not?"

Blythe had an answer, but wouldn't mention it to Myrtle. What she had to say, Tom should hear. "I'm going to take you up on your offer. Tom and I do need a heart-to-heart."

The chicken enchiladas eaten, the candles never moved from beside the vitamins, a half bottle of Chablis down her hatch, Blythe hadn't been able to coax Tom into anything.

"Say, Redd." He appeared tired. "Have you seen anything of my aftershave?"

"I poured it out."

"Oh. Well. Fine. Guess it didn't appeal to you."

"Something with a lighter bouquet would fit you better, perhaps with a woodsy scent rather than cloves. I have a brand in mind, and would be honored if you'd allow me to replace your loss, out of my own pocket." Gosh, that sounded stilted.

"Whatever."

"I'm going for a walk." She stood up from the table, tucked one of the wine bottles into the crook of her elbow and yanked down the hems of her Bermuda shorts. "I'd love it if you'd join me."

"Think I'll pass. I'm tuckered out. Too much good food and fine wine." He patted his stomach. "Think I'll turn in early."

"Channel surfing does weary the bones," she said snidely and hiked to the back door, slamming the screen as she burst into night air. What a dumb thing, thinking he might be interested in a heart-to-heart.

She walked the half mile to Sweet Creek, a trio of deer fleeing at the sight of her, before she reached the area where she and Tom had made love, so many times, so many years ago.

The scents of the grass and loam, and the gurgling water and fresh air eased her irritation, even if they did remind her of times best forgotten. A cypress tree hugged the water's edge, luring her. She settled into its cradle of knobs and rested back against the trunk. The throaty croaks of a frog snared her gaze to the tailless amphibian. The frog watched as she swallowed from the wine bottle and groused, "Sheesh."

What a hopeless case, Tom Tillman.

"I'm a headcase," Tom muttered under his breath and uncorked another bottle of wine, instead of going to bed.

He chugged a glass of Chablis. It took the edge off.

This deal with Blythe hadn't gone well, no doubt about that. He'd kept quiet about Diablo and the squeeze ball. Not once in the past two days had he mentioned missing several episodes of the soaps and Oprah. In hindsight, keeping quiet didn't sound like such a smart idea.

He poured another glass, but before finishing it, he was out the door, searching for Blythe.

Having given up on Tom, Blythe listened to the creek and wondered how it went with Mrs. Mezkat. Had the Florida lady learned any new dance steps? Did she still burn up the romance-novel boards at her online service? Had she gotten the new widower who lived two doors down to return her casserole dish?

Blythe's thoughts turned to Sir Montgomery Honeybone. Strange, not being in daily contact with Sir Monty, the middle-aged managing director of Partners in Crisis. Just as she finished pondering the oh-so-very-English nobleman, she heard the approach of a cantankerous Texan.

In a big voice that awakened a nest of wild turkeys, scattering them, Tom said, "Thought I'd find you out here."

"I didn't realize I was that predictable."

"You got a burr under your saddle, Redd?"

"Maybe I do."

He eased to the ground near her. "Want to talk about it?"

"Actually, yes." At last she could give a lucid answer. "It was foolish of me, returning to Texas."

"I'm liking your visit."

"Are you now? That's funny. I'm not getting that at

all.'' She finished off the last of the wine. ''What I'm getting is bored. *Y vent dans les voiles.*''

''That sounds nasty.''

''It means, 'And tipsy.'''

''Oh.''

From the way he slumped, she knew his feelings were hurt. Maybe it was time to hurt his feelings. He'd had enough coddling. ''I'm going to tell the truth,'' she said, the wine talking. ''I didn't think this trip through. I wanted to be a kid again for a few weeks. I see that now. I'm not the kid I used to be. Just as you aren't.''

''You may shove thorns up my toenails from time to time, but...I like you even better nowadays.''

Had wine loosened his tongue? Her own tongue continuing to wag from the fruit of the vine, she said, ''I don't like you.''

His back stiffened. ''Talk like that scares me. You must feel something along the lines of like. If you don't, why'd you show up? Don't answer that. The thing is, I don't want you to fly away again. Not without something. I'd like your friendship, at the very least.''

''You want those things, yet you don't work for what you want. You don't take chances anymore.''

A moment went by with no sounds beyond those of the creek and the night creatures.

''I fail at chance taking,'' Tom finally said, his voice quiet. ''When I quit on the rehab center, I knew my wife had been lonely too long. I was her husband. I needed to perform.'' He glanced at a spot in the darkened distance. ''I couldn't. I made her sick, just looking at me.''

Blythe hurt from hearing that. It would be callous not

to respond to his pain. She could be abrupt, yet she had a soft spot for the hurts that tear a person to shreds.

"The keyword is 'perform.' You pushed yourself, Tom. Before you were ready. It screwed up your head."

"You think so?"

"I think you need to branch out. Get yourself a horse."

"I've got one. Diablo."

"I mean a real one."

"No horses." He sliced the air with the edge of a palm. "And don't you dare bring up the subject of cattle."

"All right. No horses. No cows. You'd probably let them starve, anyway, since you don't even exercise Diablo."

"About Diablo—"

"I don't want to talk about Diablo. I want to talk about you. If this ranch were in shape... If it seemed normal around here, you'd have a better outlook. You could start small. Maybe with a goat or two. Goat milk is quite nutritious. And I could teach you to make cheese. I learned in the Middle East."

"You bet. Staked goats. That's my scene. Need I remind you? I'm not a dairy farmer. Anyhow, ranching was my second love. I had a pitching arm, you know."

Baseball, ranching. Where had love for Blythe Redd fit in? Where, for that matter, had Dana McCabe fit in? Apparently they had both been the farm league to Tom. Or staked goats. No big news, those. That empty APO box in Germany had been the first downer of a clue.

She took another swig of wine, feeling sorry for herself. She even felt a wee bit sorry for Dana. *Get serious.*

"Still got a baseball?" Blythe asked, determined to center on the here and now. "You and I could toss it back and forth."

"Forget it." He scooted closer; their knees touched. His good hand settled on her thigh. The scent of Tom, unembellished, did things to her nose that put to shame the memory-inciting scents of the creek. "Redd, I'm not beyond hope. I'm willing to take a chance. With you. I'd like to try sex therapy. Interested?"

If this was his idea of foreplay, no wonder Dana took a powder. Besides, he'd once claimed a Porsche as Blythe's best feature. "Not interested."

Starlight reflected the hurt in his eyes. "Is it that bad, coming home again?"

"China Grove isn't my home. My home is wherever I unpack my uniforms. No. I had a home with Jean-Pierre, in our hearts."

Tom rose to booted feet, turned and picked up a rock to skim across the creek. "Sounds like you really loved that hombre."

It's possible to love twice. But Tom had been her first love. Her great love. "I wouldn't have married, if I hadn't loved him."

His thumbs shoving into the back pockets of his jeans, Tom ambled down the creek bank. A few moments later he returned to Blythe. "Did you two make love before you got those rocks on your ring finger?"

So long had she worn her wedding band that it had become second skin. Why take it off? To her way of thinking, she had no reason to. She might not have called herself by Jean-Pierre's name, but she was still his widow. Maybe she should tuck the ring away, though, since she'd decided to stop grieving for him. Then again, why should she shed her second skin?

Whatever the case, the subject of Tom's question took precedence. "It's none of your business, but for friendship's sake, I'll answer. Yes, we did."

"But you won't with me."

"Right."

A second stretched taut between them. "Am I that repulsive, Redd?"

"It's not the way you look. I find you as attractive as ever. I tremble for your kisses."

"Really?"

"Really. But it's what's between the ears that makes a man truly attractive. I'm used to being dazzled. You used to dazzle me. Your dazzle has dulled."

"This is the second time you've accused me of being—what did you call it? Oh, yeah. Provincial. You're used to bullets. And men in berets."

She clicked her tongue. "You don't have a clue, do you? It's not where a man is from. It's excitement. Idealism. Goals. Determination. It's dedication to whatever makes him most terrific."

"You don't ask for much," Tom said dryly.

"I expect everything. If we worked on your libido problem, it would be sex therapy, that's all."

Even as she made that accusation, she realized if she were ever again in Tom's arms— Where was her head? Muddled from wine, or hormones or abstinence? All three? She cleared her thoughts. It would be flat nuts for them to get steamed up, then run the risk of bruising his ego.

If she were honest with him, she'd admit that there was safety in his impotence.

Never again would he have control over her body and soul.

"I don't do sex therapy," she said. "I've already told you that." Considering his feelings, she came up with an alternative. Something he could handle, if he chose to. Something they could both delight in. "What I want is the danger, the romance of dazzling."

"Roses and candlelight?"

"I'd be more impressed with dash and flash."

"Flash?" He chuckled. "Like opening my overcoat to you?"

She couldn't help but laugh. "That's a start."

"Like this?" He ripped open his shirt. Snaps crackled. Tom waved the tails as if they were wings.

Stars twinkled brighter. She could have sworn church bells rang. "You remind me of Terrific Tom." Impulsive, spur-of-the-moment. Young. Ready for action. "You still look good with your shirt open."

He went statue-like. "You're just saying that."

"When was the last time I lied to you? Never!"

"What about the masseur? That was fibbing."

"Not really. I did speak with the Swedish fellow, but thought better about hiring him. He had fishy-smelling breath." She sighed. "I'm not lying about you, Tom. And I won't. You look terrific."

He smiled. "Where have you been all these years, pussycat? You're just what I need."

A grin dragging up her cheeks, she bent to hug her knee, her ankle waving. "Do you still do your matador impersonation?"

The tails dropped. Somber, he threw his shoulders back, his head turning to the side, hands moving to the right. A graceful step backward. "Toro, toro," he growled in a lousy imitation of a Spanish accent. Waving an imaginary cape, he crooned, "*¡Andale!* I must have your ear to toss to the lovely *señorita.*"

"That's it!" It wasn't funny, his matador act, but it recalled an enjoyable page from their past. Giddiness, silliness—the perks of youth. The best part? Realizing he'd willingly bared his chest to her, even if it hadn't been to sobriety or full light. "You can still move."

"I'm trying, Redd. I am."

He reached for her hand. Once she stood, her line of sight at the tip of his nose, he gripped her waist. Oh, yes, she delighted in his long-awaited touch.

Too bad an antidote for sexual chemistry couldn't be distilled, like perfume.

"I've got a secret," he drawled. "I've been riding Diablo and squeezing that damn ball. I was going to surprise you with my prowess, once I got some."

"No joke?"

His eyes lingered on hers. "No joke."

Night became day, letting forth the light between them. Would Tom step into it? With all her soul, she hoped so.

Yet practicality yanked her into the nurse mode. "I trust you're not overdoing it. You could get tendinitis."

"I'm not getting tendinitis. I am getting some of that cardio power, though. And I drank a can of Ensuromedic today."

Chemistry at work on her fingertips, they lifted to his

triceps. Oh, he did feel good. "Then I have done some good, coming to Texas?"

"I don't know a damn thing about Texas, but you're doing me good." One fine eyebrow quirked. "I'd like to do *you* good, sweet'eart. I want you to leave here with good memories of me. Of us. Together."

This was the best news she'd heard since the last cease-fire had been announced.

At that moment his arms snaked behind her waist, bringing her closer to him. His head angled, his lips pressed. He felt warm and solid, all Tom. A heady mix. Her insides went soft, heated, even before his kiss deepened, the wine on his lips a further enticement. A flash of energy alerted her long-denied senses: this was what it felt like, having Tom reach for her!

Ambrosia.

As if starving, she relished the weight of his arms, his nearness, even the faintly sweaty scent of him. Manna to a hungry heart. It almost didn't matter, that empty APO box.

"Remember the first time we visited the creek?" he whispered against her cheek, his breath fanning her ear and eliciting a quiver. "We were tinhorns at this sort of thing. I was the first boy to kiss you. You were the first girl I'd ever kissed and meant it. Neither of us knew what the hell we were doing, making love. But we learned, didn't we? Remember the wonders of it? Remember…"

"I do. Oh, yes, I do," she answered, her voice breathy. "You were gentle at first."

"I was a bumbler before I got gentle."

"But you did find the right rhythm." My, how he'd

found it. They had both been ardent, so ardent. She recalled the time they argued over whether she'd attend the junior prom with him. She'd been adamant—she wouldn't call attention to their romance. He'd taken her roughly that night, their argument ending in rapture. "It was wonderful."

He'd later taken her to the prom, standing proudly beside her. Even when Berto Cherino and Dana McCabe had jeered at the best-looking boy "getting hooked" by the fattest girl.

"Kiss me again," he now ordered.

Their mouths met, opened, tongues tangling. Arms lifted and explored. Chests pressed together. When he kissed the slope of her throat, she murmured, "Oh, Tom. You make me dizzy. You make me forget how wrong we are for each other."

"Why're we wrong for each other? Once, we were a great fit. We could be again." He loosened his arms, cocked his head. "I mean, I can't make any promises, but I'm willing to see a doctor. I'm willing to do anything to make you happy."

Anything to make her happy. She'd heard that before, not long before he'd gone to the cheerleader who disappeared when he needed her most.

That empty APO box had been the pits.

"Did you bring Dana to this very creek?" she asked, and took a backward step. "Forget I said that. This place is handy. She replaced me. More than that, you took her as your wife. Of course you took her at Sweet Creek."

"Wrong." Tom stepped closer, his unblemished hand taking Blythe's elbow, his voice caressing her, like a gentle, balming breeze. "This place is...*was* ours. Mine and yours."

Should she believe him? Yes. The tender squeezings of emotion within her, she smiled, yet those same emotions turned on her, again reminding her that even though Sweet Creek was theirs, he had done something, somewhere with Dana.

"For both our sakes," he said, "we'd do well not to dwell on our separation."

"True, but not tonight. I need to work on getting my mind right to this."

Blythe moved away from Tom. To the house. To her borrowed room where she stayed put. "You're nuts, dragging up the past with him," she said to herself. "Sure, he did something, somewhere with that blond floozy. He was young, lusty. You expected a monk? Get real. You were no vestal virgin."

Self-castigation didn't help. She still hurt. He had married Dana. Whether by hook or by crook, he'd said, "I do."

Hours later Blythe fell to the fogged slumber of too much wine, too much emotion. Yet as those hours went by, she took more satisfaction in his admission. The creek was theirs. Theirs alone. Hers and Tom's.

Blythe awoke to a ringing. It had to be inside her head. Her ears felt as if they were attached to the outside of a bell, a big one. The ringing didn't stop.

The telephone.

Her mouth dry, she glanced at the bedside clock. Six-thirty. Too early to die of a hangover. Too late to take back last night. Just the right moment to think about a creek-side sanctuary.

Get real.

That Tom had kept the creek for them alone didn't outweigh the negatives.

"Riinnnnggg!"

"Hullo," she said with a croak, her head screaming, *Aspirin, aspirin.*

"Blythe?" Ed Saldivar said. "You're just the one I'm looking for. Can you meet me at my shop?"

She knew why. "I don't think so. I've decided not to buy Tom anything else."

"Uh-oh. Looks like I'm stuck. That's *no bueno*. I'm leaving for El Paso and need cash. I already bought—"

"I'll be there in thirty minutes." Or should she consult Tom about it? No, she knew what she was doing. She just hoped Tom would understand.

I find you attractive as ever. I tremble for your kisses. You look good with your shirt open. I've never lied to you.

Tom lay in dreamlike suspension, Blythe's words echoing in his thoughts. He waved his shirttail. She smiled her round-faced smile that melted his heart. They kissed. Here they were, in bed together.

Warm and soft in his bed, his Redd. He groaned her name. He combed fingers into her titian hair. Desire tightened on that place that hadn't tightened in years.

Again his lips opened, this time into her hair.

He tasted dog.

His eyes flew open. He yelped. The pleasurable pressure ebbed.

He shoved fox-colored fur from his bed.

Nippy landed on all fours.

Tom muttered a curse word that he hadn't uttered since age fifteen, when Granny Myrt had caught him cussing. For punishment, she had swabbed his tongue with a cake of Dial soap.

Cussing be damned. He wished Blythe had been in bed with him, where he could cuddle and caress her. Where he could soothe her hurt feelings. She needed to know. He'd given his love but once. Only to Blythe Redd.

"Got to find Redd, boyo," he said to the dog.

He rubbed his neck, glancing at the bedside clock that read 8:00 a.m. His gaze caught on the bed's unused pillow. His remote control rested atop it. His *chewed up* remote control.

Tom repeated that Dial-worthy word and spat a strand of dog hair from his tongue.

Great, just great.

Why wasn't it truly great? He'd finally gotten the nerve last night to go for broke with Blythe. While the results weren't roses and candlelight, she hadn't been altogether discouraging. All right, she hadn't seemed too impressed that he'd kept the creek sacred to them, but she could have a change of heart on that.

And he had awakened with an arousal.

Tom smiled. "Hallelujah, Slugger still works."

Whistling a tune, he dropped the remote control into the trash, went to the bathroom for what Granny Myrt called ablutions and stepped into the shower. He could do dash and flash.

He dressed in a cowboy's best version of dash and

flash, a long-sleeved yoked shirt of royal blue and a pair of dry-cleaner-pressed jeans. He even found his newest pair of ropers, and wiped the dust off them.

Nippy watching him, he said, "I'm in the mood for pancakes. Blythe likes pancakes. I'll make a batch, fry up some bacon. We can have a nice breakfast. It might lead to some dashing and flashing."

Nippy cocked his head.

Whoa, Tillman. Think this situation through.

"She's got ideas along the dazzle line. Can I hold that line? Getting her interest and keeping it will take major efforts, inside and out. Too much work. Besides, I don't want to work. All I care about is a big bossy redhead who doesn't know when to quit."

But Blythe followed dreams. She expected the same out of him. His only dream being the bossy redhead, he wondered how much he'd be willing to give, to deliver the impression of going along with her dreams.

"I'll wing it," he said to Nippy.

Trouble was, he couldn't find Blythe.

He didn't lay eyes on Shelly, either, but did find a message explaining her departure to "the Laundromat." Granny Myrt's washing machine hadn't worked in months. "I'll call the repairman," he said and did.

Tom ate alone. Well, Nippy joined him. By the time the Pomeranian had scarfed up the last piece of bacon and he and the master of the house had had a man-to-man about respecting other people's property, Tom knew he could do some winging.

He downed a glass of orange juice, then went to the porch, where he contemplated a ride on Diablo. Too hot. Well, maybe not. Just as he decided this would be the perfect morning for a feisty mustang, Tom both heard and saw the approach of two vehicles. A sporty red one and what looked to be Ed Saldivar's aged minivan a good deal behind it. Pulling a horse trailer.

Night crawlers of intuition wormed up Tom's spine. Any thoughts of making up for the creek vanished.

A feeling much akin to a hangover settled in his head and stomach. Ed wasn't here to look for his daughter. That horse trailer meant something, and knowing Blythe, Tom had a good guess what that something meant.

This would be a good time to duck into the house.

Some nameless force within Tom—probably survival, possibly murder!—nailed his ropers to the porch floor.

The sports car halted, swirling gravel at its tail. Ms. Sunny Delight emerged from the interior, grinning. Short curls and ear hoops bounced, as did her bosom. She waved gaily, even though she looked a tad peaked.

"You'll never guess what I bought," she called.

Hands clenched at his sides, he un-nailed the ropers and legged it over to get in her face. Sweat popping on his brow, he tried to ignore the scent of erotic perfume that drifted to his nostrils like a siren's call. "You don't value your life."

She raised her wrist to indicate an inch between her thumb and index finger. "It's just a teeny-tiny little something."

"I wouldn't bet on that."

"You look fantastic today." Obviously she played for time. "Nice clothes. That shirt sets off the blue in your eyes."

"*¡Hola, amigos!*" came Ed's voice as he rolled out of the van. Wiping his palms down the bow of a formidable gut, he started toward Tom and Blythe. "Hot day, isn't it? But it's a fine day for living!"

Where were those pecans when Tom needed them?

Blythe took his left hand in a grip that brooked no stalling, then marched him forward. "I've been telling Tom about the surprise."

"Come see, *amigo*." Ed stopped, arced a beefy arm and pointed toward the trailer. "Come see!"

A beast let out a neigh. A time-whitened gray muzzle poked between trailer slats. Equine lips peeled back to let forth a nicker that exposed long, yellowed teeth.

Tom feared he'd seen those exact teeth before. That horse looked way too familiar. Blythe kept marching and dragging. His knees trembled. He tried to think of a way to kill her and get away with it.

Ed unlatched the trailer's gate, set down the ramp, then went inside to collect the dubious surprise.

First a long neck, a straggling gunmetal-gray mane growing from the crest of it, protruded from the confines, followed by the rest of an indeed recognizable mare. If yelling weren't the wussy thing to do, if perfect murder didn't elude him, Tom would have been guilty of both.

That was Pickles, sure as sin.

Prudence Packard had first owned the gray mare, before she'd sold it to Nestor Cantu. Nestor's quartet of evil-minded daughters later bilked schoolkids out of lunch money to ride on that swayed back.

Avoiding eye contact with Blythe, Tom gave thanks she didn't utter one word, much less a syllable. *Let this be some sort of joke.*

"Ed," Tom said, his voice cracking like a raven's, "tell me you don't take MasterCard."

Chapter Six

One would have thought Blythe had butchered a beloved house pet or been mean to babies or created mayhem at the Happy Acres Retirement Home, so much did Tom give a cold shoulder over Pickles.

His attitude worsened her headache.

He refused to speak to her, even when they retreated from Ed and entered Tom's house. She said, "Pickles is mine. I knew you wouldn't appreciate her. So I bought her for myself." True enough. "Ed Saldivar paid cash for the mare—he couldn't get a refund. The Saldivars can't afford to keep Pickles. Does that make me evil?"

"There are names for women like you. One being Easy Mark."

"Would you stop walking away? I haven't committed a crime."

Short of the hallway, Tom glanced over his shoulder. "Okay, fine. Now what are you going to do with her?"

"I was hoping you'd help me with her."

"You would." Tom went to his room and slammed the door shut.

"What a guy," she seethed.

Blythe had to get Pickles stabled.

It had been years since she'd touched horseflesh, and even though docile described Pickles, getting her groomed, fed and settled in weren't the easiest of tasks. Thankfully, Shelly, once she returned from the washateria, lent a hand.

Blythe's lapsed hero continued the silent treatment. The washer-fixer guy arrived, and left. Tom turned his nose up at the tuna casserole Shelly prepared for lunch, as well as the chicken she roasted for dinner, before leaving for the night. He kept to his room even after Myrtle blew in from school.

After finding out about Pickles, Myrtle said, "Uh-oh. I ain't gonna stick around. Think I'll drive out to Prudence Packard's place. See if she's got any of that coffee cake she makes special. Maybe I'll get me a room at Donna Scott's motel for the night. Can I borrow your car? I always did wanna strike a pose next to a fancy red Hupmobile."

As soon as the Porsche's tires had stirred dust, Blythe took two more aspirins and approached Tom's bedroom to tap on the wooden door. "Can we talk?" Several heartbeats later, she asked, "How long do you intend to pout?"

"I'm not pouting," he replied, the sound muffled by the door that kept them apart. Or shouldn't she accept that *she* had put up a barrier much more solid than wood?

"May I come in?" She was determined not to sound hesitant.

"It's not locked."

She entered the darkened, book-crammed room. Remarkably, Tom switched on a lamp. The flood of light didn't reach his eyes.

Amid those dusty books, he was lodged in an overstuffed chair, his ankles crossed on an ottoman. A coterie of empty glasses and TV schedules littered the table also holding the lamp and its yellowed shade. Shirt and jeans rumpled, his hair going this way and that, he looked like five miles of bad road.

Hoping to avoid a pitched battle, she asked, "Have you read all these books?"

"Not lately." His gaze aimed for hers, pitching battle. "It wasn't bad enough, the massage or Diablo. You had to bring that old nag onto the Sweet Creek. And charge her to me!"

"That's not so." Blythe approached the iron bed, sat near Tom's chair. "Like he said, Ed does take credit cards at his car repair shop. But I paid by check. Pickles would've been my gift to you, if you hadn't looked a gift horse in the mouth."

"If this is the part where I'm supposed to say, 'thank you,' keep talking."

"You see, I asked Ed a few days ago to find a horse. One I could afford. I had no idea he thought I was destitute."

"I may be in worse shape than the gray, but, dammit, if I were to saddle up again—which I have no intention of doing—what makes you think I'd make a fool of myself?" Tom humphed. "Ride a mount that carried first-graders across the Dairy Divine parking lot? I'm insulted."

"Ed says Pickles is a fine horse for short rides. Besides, if you got used to riding again, you could buy your own mount. Buy the Kentucky Derby winner, if that's what suits you."

"You didn't even give me a chance to get Diablo broken to the bit, before you pushed me into something else."

"All right. I was hasty. Patience has never been my long suit." Nor was forgiveness, she realized, but decided not to think about that. "Anyhow, Pickles is mine. I'll ride her."

"I'll turn you in to the A.S.P.C.A. You'd break that poor thing's spine."

Blythe blinked, hurt. "Point taken. And so much for last night's sugar talk."

"I didn't mean it that way." Tom tried to loop an arm around her shoulders, the gesture rejected. "Anyone could break Pickles's back. She's old. And about last night—"

"Enough." Fed up, Blythe quit the bed. "Think I'll check on my horse."

She set out for the little-used stable, passing the little-used barn, muttering to the night wind about sticks and stones. "I'm made of better stuff than touchiness. Besides, he's a sourpuss. Consider the source."

When she reached the stable, she noted the six stalls and large tack room. Cobwebs and dilapidation were everywhere. It needed attention, same as its owner.

The stable had been much in use, when Tom's maternal grandfather owned the Sweet Creek. After Grandpa Rogers passed to a greater reward, Tom's father cried "won't" and took off for a job on an offshore drilling rig. For weeks on end, he'd left a ten-year-old in charge. Ably. It made a man out of Tom, those responsibilities at a tender age. Furthermore, he got acquainted with hammers and nails, although one would never guess that now.

Currycomb in hand, Blythe entered Pickles's stall, approached the mare, and began to groom gray-haired hide. "When we were teenagers, Tom did more than keep outbuildings in repair. He never made cruel remarks."

Pickles, snorting her approval, leaned into the comb, grateful for her massage.

"No more dash and flash for Terrible Tom, no sirree, bob. Which is just as well, now that I think about it. I refuse to end up in a straitjacket. But…Pickles, what am I going to do? He's a rat." Deep into her pity party, Blythe sniffed. "He's hateful, remarking on my weight."

Neck curved, Pickles eyed Blythe, then peeled back her lips, displaying decades of tooth growth. Obviously she sided with Blythe.

"There're three kinds of men in this world. The ones who don't mind extra weight. The ones who say they don't, but leave chunky women to the first kind. Then there're the ones who simply aren't interested. I'm not interested in the last two types. There are enough of the first to go around." But no other man had her interest, and she couldn't imagine finding anyone else to thrum her strings.

"Redd," the object of her thoughts said from outside, from over the Dutch door's top. "I've always been interested in you."

She dropped the comb. "Wh-what're you doing, eavesdropping?"

"Clearing up a misconception." Tom opened the half door, crooked a finger and urged her outdoors. "The creek. Now!"

"I'm not going to the creek with you," she said, meaning it. "We're up the creek already, so to speak."

"Grab a paddle, Redd. If you think I've got something against your weight, you're going down for the third time."

She couldn't help admiring the golden highlights of his hair as moonbeams hit it. *You slug, get over him.* "I can paddle on my own."

Tom hitched a thumb away from the stable, toward the home place. "Let's talk in the house."

"I've got cabin fever." Or the need for mind-bending drugs. Stepping outside, she closed the lower half of Pickles's stall door. The latch slipped; it took two tries to secure it. "I'm in the mood for a root beer float. I'm going to Dairy Divine."

"You eat too much junk food."

"What sweet talk."

"I told you I need help."

"Yeah, well. You're a fine one to give advice. Besides, I plan to order diet and yogurt."

"Do you now?" He shifted from one leg to the other

and dug into his pocket, just before clouds moved under the moon.

Church bells rang.

"Make you a deal," he said. "When we get to Nestor's, you dash in, flash this ten-spot of mine and order a couple root beer floats. We'll drive over to the ball field and slurp 'em up."

"Been there, done that with the ball park. We'll sit under the front canopy at Dairy Divine."

Clouds parted. He was handing her the ten-dollar bill. "I suggest we dash to the pickup and be off in a flash."

"You've got a date."

She knew he couldn't dash, but they were, for all intents and purposes, off in a flash, with the Tillman pickup nosed toward town. It had been a long time since a man, beyond cabbies or transport drivers, drove Blythe anywhere; she enjoyed sitting back and gazing at Tom's profile. He had a nice profile. Strong, with the marks of good Texas pioneer stock.

In the dark he almost looked like the old Tom, young and unblemished.

Her headache vanished.

They passed the church, the taxidermy shop, the Woof Clipper salon, Fill-Er-Fast, Happy Acres Retirement Home, the Scott Motel, the industrial bakery that made tasty goodies of the lower end variety. They last traveled by Ron Dinlum's vacant automobile agency, the latter where the reunion would be held. The sidewalks were empty.

Tom steered the pickup beneath the drive-in's canopy.

Blythe heard him exhale in relief. No need to wonder

why. Nary another car or pickup occupied the lot. No customers for Nestor. No prying eyes to gawk at Tom.

Blythe dashed in and got the floats.

"This doesn't taste like diet or yogurt," her date commented once they sipped through straws.

"Imagine that."

"Redd?"

"Nestor makes the best root beer floats in China Grove."

"He makes the only root beer floats in China Grove."

"Would've been a crime to ask him to lower the sugar or saturated fat levels."

"You said last night you don't lie to me."

"A lot got said last night. But I didn't lie about the floats. I just changed my mind before ordering. Do you think you might change...well, never mind. Does it bother you, Pickles using your stable for now?"

He slanted a gaze at her. "I don't mind. She can stay, as long as you're here."

"Thank you."

"Just keep in mind, I said 'as long as you're here.'"

Somehow Blythe couldn't imagine leaving. Which scared her. What's the deal? she asked herself. Staying wasn't part of her plan. She chose to think of herself as a good Samaritan, a nurse who would help a friend's emotional recovery and take pleasure in his rehabilitation. They would not end up lovers; for that she was thankful.

Of course, she hadn't planned to fall for Tom again.

How far had she fallen?

Best not to study him, or think too deeply on that

question. Or on why she had ever considered him a
friend, after he'd totally avoided her for fifteen years.

She craned her neck to see around Tom. "There's
Shelly," she said, relieved at an interruption. "That
must be her boyfriend she's with. Myrtle doesn't like
him. Ikey."

"Icky. Icky Kuleska." Tom eyeballed the teenage
couple who got out of an airbrushed TransAm and were
veering off course for Dairy Divine's entrance, making
for the pickup. "Damn."

"Hey, Blythe. Tom. How y'all doin'?" Shelly, her
hair "screamin'" as Myrtle had tagged it, scrunched
down to wave into the truck cab. "Nice night, isn't it?
Nice but hot."

The pale young man, Icky, bopped up. With a billed
cap—not the "gimme" kind often favored in Texas—
shading one side of his goateed face, he jammed his
thumbs into the waistband of blousy knee-shorts. Any
more jamming, and those shorts would go south.

The forearm he rested on Tom's opened window bore
the tattoo Born To Raiz Hell.

"Feel the heat. Can't retreat. Heat's got the ice. Make
the 'hood pay the price. Feel the heat." Icky clamped
his attempt at rhymes to stick his face close to Tom's.
Opal studs lined his ear. "Man, you look like the heat
done iced you. That's one bahddd-lookin' scar."

"Shut up, Icky," Shelly demanded. "Mom says it's
not nice to say anything about... Tom is a hero, you
know." She waved at Blythe and Tom, and yanked the
boy toward Dairy Divine.

Already Tom had set his float in a drink holder, ready
to turn the ignition. Blythe laid her fingertips across his

trembling knuckles. "Don't. The time for hiding is over."

His hand fell away from the key. "Is it?"

"If you can't change the way you look, change the way you think."

"Tough assignment."

"If it were easy, everyone would be happy."

"I don't know where to start."

"Make a daily affirmation. 'I've got my mind right enough, and if people don't like my looks, they can look elsewhere. And, by golly, I'm smart enough not to wear baggy shorts or to concoct lousy poetry.'"

Tom laughed with good humor. "You're crazy, Redd. Totally nutty. Crazy-nutty wonderful."

"Tell me something I don't know," she rejoined, smiling, assessing his straight nose and sturdy chin, her finger kicking up a lock of his golden hair.

"Something you don't know? Here goes." He motioned toward Dairy Divine's interior, to Icky. "Did you know that lad wants to become a rap star?"

"Scary."

"Yeah, it is. Did you also know Shelly's writing a book about you?"

"You're kidding."

"I'm not. She's reached page five."

"I'm honored."

"You should be. Wonder how it'll end?"

Blythe took a plastic spoon to the melted ice cream at the top of her float. "I imagine with something dramatic, that is if she wants to make a bestseller out of it."

"Like with you getting hit by a bullet?" Tom

scratched his earlobe with a thumbnail. "Or with the ladder breaking as you climb into a hovering helicopter?"

"Killjoy. Fatalist."

"Goes with the territory."

His newly darkened attitude put her off the best root beer float in China Grove. She took hers, plus the one he'd abandoned, and got out of the truck to toss the drinks in a nearby trash can.

Tom was in the dumps. Of course, being here at Dairy Divine with Blythe had had its good moments, but he couldn't stop thinking about the look that kid had given him, couldn't stop thinking about Blythe twisting in the wind.

Maybe he did need to get his mind right enough, like she'd suggested.

He watched her walk back to the pickup. She seemed so sure of herself, so confident. She was those things. Her travels had taken her over more than continents. She was truly at one with Blythe Redd.

She slid onto the seat and closed the door. "Tom, I've been thinking about territory. You and China Grove have seen too much of each other. You need a change of scenery. Why don't we drive over to Houston and buy a pair of tickets to the Astros game?"

"Redd, I gave up baseball when I married. Furthermore—"

"Why?"

"Too much trouble."

"My, what a startling revelation."

"Yeah, well, that's the way of my world. And I do *not* want to show my face in the Astrodome. Got it?"

"Clear as mud."

"Don't look at me like that, Redd, with disgust in your eyes, that nose of yours in the air, like you're smelling something putrid. Think about this. Isn't it said a person can't run from his troubles, that it follows him?"

"I'm not looking at you like that." She stretched an arm atop the seat back. "Revert to the affirmation, sir. Do not pass Go, do not collect the C-notes. Do it."

The affirmative. The just-do-it mentality. He could try, since he had something to say. Grinning—sheepishly, no doubt—he sloped his jaw toward her expectant face then turned back to profile. As he glanced at her again, the grin probably appearing as dumb and uncertain as he felt at the moment, he admitted, "Looks like I'm not impotent."

"Really?"

Hers wasn't exactly the reply he'd expected. It didn't do anything to bolster his flagging ego. "Well, you don't have to look as if I've sent Pickles to the taxidermy shop."

"I'm pleased for you. Honestly." She licked her lips. "But it throws a shoe in the works. I'm not here for sex or sex therapy. If you're thinking you can cajole me straight out of my panties, think again."

While he had the urge to duck her statement to save face as well as feelings, he wouldn't. His hand cruised across her knee. "I did have that in mind."

"Whoa." The arm that had been parked atop the seat now lifted. She waved, as if protecting her space. "Hold the plane. I thought we settled it. No sex therapy."

"I thought you'd be happy for me," he said, the ache of rejection going through him. "Don't let it trouble you, Redd. I won't force you into a..." What should he call it? "Just forget I mentioned it. I just thought I might look into some flashing and dashing that might end up in the old way."

He wanted to feel like a man again, to feel just for a little while what he had felt with Blythe when he was young, whole and terrific.

Tom started the pickup and peeled out of Dairy Divine.

Blythe didn't know what to say. She stared out the pickup window on the drive from Dairy Divine. Answers wouldn't come from gawking at darkened scenery. She glanced at Tom's profile, his features illuminated by the night lights of a small town.

"I don't want to end up in the old way," she announced.

"I figured you could handle whatever happened. You are a sophisticated woman who buzzes around, hanging from helicopters. What you see is what you get with me. But we do have a history."

She sighed at hearing herself called sophisticated. To someone from the backwater of China Grove, anything above Bulgarian eau de toilette or American-made vehicles lent a certain élan. No way would she correct him.

"History or not, I don't want an affair. All ours did was break my heart."

He pulled to the side of the road, cut the engine. Leaning toward her, he said, "Why in the name of hell did you come back here then?"

"To help you."

"Why?"

"Because…because—" *I am not going to cry. I'm not going to do it.* "If you're what you used to be, good and caring, then I'll atone for…"

"For what?" He took her hand.

"For not loving my husband the way he should have been loved." The words were out before Blythe could call them back. Why had she told him the secret truth of her marriage?

Tom tugged her into his arms and laid her head against his shoulder. He patted her, stroked her back. Gave her strength. "If you loved him at all," he whispered, "then your Frenchman was a lucky man."

She sniffed back a tear and looked up at Tom. "That's a strange thing for a man to say about another man."

A sad yet teasing smile played over his handsome, scarred face. "Sweet'eart, maybe I'm just different."

"Yes, I think you are."

She lifted her lips to Tom's, rejoicing in the taste and feel of him, giving in to the impulse to kiss and be kissed without second thought. Yet she was glad when he pulled away, before reminding her what could be, if they allowed it.

Tom stretched like an old cat, no doubt like a feeble-minded tom, even though Diablo bucked. This day, the morning after the Dairy Divine, the bright sun was chasing cotton puffs of clouds. He felt magnificent. "Giddap, you devil!"

Blythe not only burst onto the porch, she also burst

his bubble. "Shelly didn't show up for work this morning. I called her house. She's not there."

Tom stopped spurring to study the worry in the world's prettiest face. "She probably got something going with Icky."

"Margaret says Shelly left a vague note about San Antonio plans." Nervous fingers twisted an ear hoop. "It's not like Shelly, being undependable."

Concern mounted Tom's spine; he whipped off his sunglasses. A couple of days after Shelly pointed out Blythe's pluses and Tom's minuses, the girl asked his opinion on teenage marriage. He'd *thought* he'd gotten through to her in their second heart-to-heart chat.

No need to upset Blythe over a hunch.

"Margaret's driving into San Antonio to look for Shelly." Blythe worried an ear hoop to death. "I said we'd watch Nippy."

"Joy to the world." Beyond his sarcastic remark, Tom bit down on clutching guilt. *I should've paid more attention to the girl.*

"Hell, Redd, why borrow trouble?" he asked, not one to be a sucker to sentiments. "I'm done with taking on other people's problems."

Blythe looked at him with such disgust that he almost flinched. "Is that so?" she said.

"You warned me you climb molehills. You're doing that with Shelly. I don't see the big deal. I bet she and Icky just want some time alone. That's kids for you. We were the same. They probably went to San Marcos to watch Ralph the Swimming Pig."

Shaking her head, Blythe wandered to the end of the porch, where she snapped off a dead frond from an airplane plant that hung from the rafters. "I'm not so sure Shelly and Icky hared off to San Marcos. Margaret said Shelly hasn't been herself lately. I've noticed it, too. Something's fishy."

"From Margaret's mouth to God's ears."

Blythe sent a laser-sharp glare to Tom. "You really don't win any points, constantly criticizing my choice in companions."

Why argue over companions or an elusive teenager? "That was a nice kiss we shared last night."

"Oh, hush. I can't think about kisses, not when I'm upset over Shelly."

His gaze on Blythe's lips, he said, "Make you a deal. If Shelly doesn't turn up soon, I promise to get antsy. But let's not waste this morning. Humor me, pussycat. Give me another kiss."

Hands going to her hips, Blythe announced, "Forget it."

"Can't." Tom alit the steel horse and legged over to her. His amble had gotten better, day by day. He ran his thumb along her bottom lip. "After all, I've got my mind right enough. And people can kiss my grits, by golly. Besides, I'm working on being smart enough not to wear baggy shorts or to spout lousy poetry. I need a kiss."

She swallowed; he watched her throat work as she did it.

"Hmm?" He flicked her earring with his tongue.

"Don't do that. It's bad on my knees. That's one of a plus-size woman's greatest fears, you know. Getting weak in the knees, where she can't support her weight."

"My flash and dash must've improved, if Ms. Vault the Porch is uneasy." He roped his arms behind her waist, bringing her closer to sniff the erotic scents of a worldly woman. "How am I doing? On the improvements, that is."

"About a *C*-minus." Blythe backed up and started to scoot around him. "Pickles needs exercise. You need exercise. Get back on Diablo. I think you can add a minute to your schedule without tempting tendinitis."

"Not so fast." He swung her around; they ended up with him sideways on Diablo's saddle, Blythe on his lap, which was expanded gloriously. Gloriously in his estimation, anyhow.

"Why do you sit the fence, when it's me and you?" he wanted to know. "We're adults. We're unencumbered. We've done this sort of thing before...together."

She squirmed. His hold tightened, while his pulse raced. It no longer bothered him, touching or being touched. Funny, what Blythe could do.

But could he go the distance? An arousal didn't mean... Well, she didn't want his loving and he wouldn't make her. He would, nonetheless, give in to his urges to tease her.

"Tell me, sweet'eart. Guide me on the right path to more dash and flash." The tip of his tongue bypassed gold to lap the lobe of her delicious ear again. "What's holding you back?"

"Because..."

He liked this hesitation in her. "Because, why?"

Her green gaze fastened to the blue of his, she said, "I don't know what to make of you. You were a hero. You're not beyond hope, I think. But you're so angry. Yet I keep thinking about how you saved the creek for me and you, and how you almost gave your life for little girls."

He didn't want to think about that, much less discuss the Cherino sisters. "Some things are sacred, like the creek."

"Yes, I know. But what about those little girls?"

"I'll tell you in good time. I can't now. Try to understand, Redd. I know you hate mysteries. If you can't stand the mystery of me, then talk to Margaret or my granny. But let me deal with myself as I must. Please."

She rested her hand against his cheek, covering the scar in what he took as a symbolic gesture, and smiled with all her warmth and understanding. "I'll wait for you to tell me."

"Do you think I could have a kiss in the meantime?"

Blythe wound her arms around Tom's neck, and he hugged her tightly, his lips finding hers. She tasted like orange juice, smelled like heaven and was a dream come true. He could get ridiculous about this woman.

Something told him he already was.

Chapter Seven

"**Y**ou ain't eat a bite of your dinner."

"I'm not much hungry, Myrtle."

"That's a first," Tom put in, obviously teasing.

He was grinning. Yet Blythe wasn't up to grinning. She was a mess.

This had not been the best of days. The evening didn't seem too promising, either, with her uneasiness over Tom and with other considerations. Shelly hadn't returned. A visit to the manicurist this afternoon hadn't gone well, although Blythe's fingernails hadn't suffered for it.

Primarily, she wondered where this situation with Tom would end up.

On the verge of primal-scream therapy, while sitting in the parlor with Tom and his grandmother, eating a TV dinner off a TV tray, listening to more television than she ever wanted to hear, Blythe stared at an entertainment show.

A vacuous-looking TV blonde with big teeth reported that some movie star's career was ruined over a thirty-pound weight gain. A rearend view of the star showed a fanny jiggling down the beach at Malibu. "Movie producer Oliver Rockford has fired Ms. Jones from *Alaska Adventure*," yapped Ms. Big Teeth.

"Ain't that your friend, that Rockford feller? Tom, cut the TV off. Honey girl, have you called Rockford about me?"

Tom walked to the TV and punched the Off button, as Blythe replied, "Not yet. Soon. Why don't we listen to some records?" she asked, forgetting the record player had long gone.

Returning to his recliner, Tom took a big bite of ravioli. "I could turn on the radio."

"I can't wait to get to Hollywood," Myrtle said. "Gonna buy me one of them CD players. Anyone for a game of dominoes?"

"No," Tom said.

Blythe swallowed iced tea. "I haven't played dominoes in years. Not since I beat two Mexican prizefighters out of a thousand pesos on the train between Oaxaca and Mexico City."

Tom gave her a strange look.

"I once played strip dominoes," Myrtle offered. "Me and Prudence, back when we was young and feisty. There was a couple of fellers from Fort Sam Houston. We dated them. It was their idea, the dominoes. I'll never forget my guy. A cavalry man. Drove a Packard. Rode a horse called Zephyr. He was some kinda sexy."

"Pulleeezze," moaned Tom.

"Once I get to Hollywood, I'm gonna get me a young feller, just like Horace. Only I want his name to be something like Blade or Rex or Rafe. Did y'all hear that?" Myrtle leaned an ear toward the door. "I swear, I think I hear a horse."

Blythe shoved the tray away and jumped up. She had indeed heard a horse. "Pickles is out of her stall."

Tom's lips twisted. "At least we won't have to hear any more dominoes stories."

Out the door in giant steps, Tom behind her, Blythe chased the old gray mare in the waning sunlight. Pickles sidestepped them both, then took off. Even Blythe was winded by the time they got the errant gray back in her stall.

"Evil girl," Blythe puffed. "You can move fast for an oldster."

"Damn, Redd. I do believe you're human."

"What...do you...mean by that?"

"You're out of breath."

"I am not. I'm just a little...overcome."

"You're sweating."

"*You* are sweating, mister, so watch your mouth." Her hip against the Dutch door, holding it closed, Blythe took a breath and ordered, "Get a screwdriver, Tom. Fix this door."

He moved like molasses.

But he got the latch reattached.

Blythe pushed away, spread her hands over her knees and breathed through her nose, then gave Pickles a warning shake of her finger before turning to Tom. "You should do repair work around here. I don't want the roof falling in on my horse.''

His spine to the outer wall of the stables, Tom slid to the ground. ''You want repairs? Fine. I'll hire a carpenter.''

''Then do it.''

''My, aren't we in a fine mood? Must've been the TV dinner. I know you like restaurants. I wish I could take you to one. Several. Dozens.''

''You can walk. You eat. Why can't we go to a restaurant?''

''If I have to answer that, then you're dumb as a box of rocks. I know you're not dumb. What's nettling you, Redd?''

She slid down next to him. ''I ran into Ted Acheson today.'' Ted had been a football star at their school. ''He's an attorney now. He was having his nails done. Gave me a coupon for a complimentary can of diet drink his wife sells.''

Tom grasped her hand. ''You got your feelings hurt.''

''I'm not myself, I guess. I am worried about Shelly.'' *And us.* ''Anyway, Ted's wife sashayed in. She's pretty, with ideal curves. But she's dumb as those rocks you mentioned. The disgusting part was, Ted is so proud of her that I wanted to puke. Superficial toad.''

''I'm proud of you. What does that make me?''

Blythe chuckled. ''Probably a one in a million guy. Definitely Terrific Tom, even if you are lazy. You're too good for China Grove. When I go to town, I get nothing but stares. Except for Ted's burnt offering of that diet drink. When people don't have anything to worry about but the size of a woman's behind, then those people need to get lives.''

"Ted isn't the whole town."

"China Grove was never kind to me. I'll be glad to leave," she added. He flinched. She then realized how brutal that had sounded. China Grove was, after all, his hometown.

"No Dutch door is keeping you stabled," he said.

Leaving might be for the best. She knew that it was just a matter of time before he would strip her panties and defense mechanisms. And then what would happen?

"I won't strap you down, Redd. So go."

Her heart thunked. She didn't want to lose him. Didn't want to go off forever, with no chance of seeing Tom again. "If I went, how do you see us, say, a year from now?"

"I don't." He ratcheted to stand. Staring at the setting sun, his back to her, he said, "You're looking for dedication and idealism, and the rest of the qualities you find attractive. I'm just me. I'm not your man."

That was it. The truth. Why did it have to hurt so much? With Tom she had hurt too much and too often. It must have been a masochistic bent that brought her to Sweet Creek Ranch. Was it the nasty ache to give as she'd gotten that kept her here?

She hoped not.

"What about the reunion?" she asked.

"You don't want to go any more than I do, if I'm reading the cards right."

"There is that. But, actually, I do have a reason for attending. I want to see who else has gotten fat."

"That's cruel.''

"I just want to see if anyone has had to pay for being cruel to me."

He laughed. "Well, sweet'eart, as you say, there is that."

She laughed, too.

He winked. "We're a fine pair of misfits, aren't we?" Tom walked to her, lifted her chin with the crook of a finger. "We've got a couple weeks or so on our hands, between now and the reunion. Want to make the most of it? No strings attached?"

There it was, another sexual invitation. She said, "I think it might be best if I spend my time taking care of Pickles."

His left thumb behind a belt loop, his right hand at his side, Tom watched Blythe lead Pickles from her stall, the pair walking into a stand of elms and mesquites, their direction the creek. He ambled back to the house.

He wished he could make her happy.

Hell, what about making himself happy?

Where was Nippy when he needed mano-a-mano?

Truth was, he hadn't been this happy, strange though that might seem, in a long time. Blythe was good for him. He'd like to be good for her.

"I could love him, Pickles. Maybe I do already. Maybe it's just hormones and abstinence. I shouldn't fall in love with Tom again. I might get ideas to stay put. A lifetime of Dairy Divine and small-town boredom? No way. I'm going to do as planned, get him to the reunion. Then I'm out of here."

Pickles reared her neck, neighing with feminine sympathy, faithful girlfriend personified. Or was it horse-ified?

Blythe patted a bony shoulder. "Which brings me to the big question. What am I going to do with you?"

A tail swished, its leading edges thwacking Blythe's arm.

"I'll think of something." Blythe watched the old girl lap a long drink of creek water. "I don't suppose you'd be interested in hearing... What if I took Tom with me?"

Pickles was done with girl talk. Blythe kept talking.

"What would he do, if he went off with me? He's not up to the rigors, nor would his heart be in it. And he's not trained in medicine. I doubt he'd make a good admin weeny. He certainly wouldn't work out as an armed guard. He never even liked to hunt or fish. And the cavalry, in essence, pretty much went out with Black Jack Pershing. Or with Horace Whatzisname. Maybe Tom could drive an ambulance."

Ridiculous. Blythe could barely get him off the ranch, much less behind the wheel of an ambulance. And he wanted no strings.

"Pickles, this is the pits. I don't know what I want."

As it turned out, getting Tom mobile wasn't that far off. Noontime the next day, Blythe received a telephone call from Margaret, a message that had a dark aura to it, like the clouds that tinted today's sky to slate.

Shelly had indeed disappeared.

Blythe set the telephone earpiece back in its cradle, then turned her eyes to Tom, who manned the kitchen sink. "Margaret thinks Shelly ran off with Icky. That boy purloined his mother's purse as well as her credit cards. Shelly cleaned out her bank savings account. I told you she was up to something fishy!''

Tom, who'd chosen to do breakfast dishes after serving pancakes and bacon, rinsed the frying pan. His face went the hue of the sky beyond the kitchen window. He glanced outside and said in a voice that also had a dark tinge to it, ''Does Margaret have any idea where they're headed?''

''She doesn't, but I do.'' Blythe went to her room, made a long-distance call, then returned with a Big Chief tablet. ''I found this. There's a phone number written on it. I've already checked it out. It's a motel in Houston. Icky is registered.''

''Damn. Double damn.''

''What does that mean?''

''It's a swear word, usually considered crass, if not rude.''

''Don't be a smart-aleck. Do you know something I don't?''

Tom rubbed his neck. ''They may want to get married.''

''Shelly's just sixteen. Icky's barely eighteen.''

''I said 'want.' Redd, they can't get married without parental permission.''

''You never heard of fake ID? Anything could happen. Margaret's worried sick. And so am I. I'm going to Houston.''

''Redd, Shelly is the Saldivars' business. If anyone hares off to Houston, it should be Margaret or Ed. Or both.''

''Ed's in El Paso, horse trading. Margaret's scared to

leave the house, for fear of missing Shelly's call. Of course, she could forward her calls out here, and I could go with her. You could wait by the telephone. But there's Pickles.''

"Don't look at me like that, Blythe Redd. I'm not—repeat, not!—going to feed that candidate for the dog food factory.''

"Dog food factory? You beast! Best I don't leave her to you. You might sell her to one.''

"Could happen.''

An idea popped. "Wait! I'll call Myrtle at school and ask her to feed Pickles.''

"Get Nestor to shove oats down her gullet.'' Tom dried his hands on a tea towel. "He owes us, after pawning that nag off on you and Ed.''

"True.'' Blythe went to the phone and eventually got Nestor Cantu's agreement. After ringing off, she said to Tom, "The only thing left to worry about is Nipster. You'll have to take him in.''

"Forget it.'' Tom looked as if he'd just gotten a root canal sans Novocain, or worse. "I'm out of house shoes and remote controls. No telling what he'd chew up next.''

"With a friend like you, who needs an enemy.''

He scowled. "All right. I give. What do you want?''

"Here are your options,'' she said. "Margaret and I go to Houston, and you dog-sit. Or...'' Blythe dreaded expressing the other option. "Or Margaret stays here, and you and I go to Houston.''

"Let me get my hat. Where are my sunglasses? Hope I haven't lost 'em. They've been missing for days.''

Blythe didn't want Tom on the trip. All that nearness.

All that angst and testosterone. All that dash and flash business. All those memories of a special creek and two rescued sisters.

He went about packing.

Hang it all.

At least he wouldn't be watching TV and feeling sorry for himself. Her goal to keep him moving, she couldn't do as Tom had done, and look a gift horse in the mouth.

A stash of cash and credit cards tucked in his wallet, Tom and Blythe drove away from the ranch in her car. She'd dressed in the capri pants and scoop-neck top he'd first eyed the day of her return. This time around they looked even better to him. Must be all his returned libido. No. It was Blythe alone.

"We need petrol and a map," she said. "Let's stop at Fill-Er-Fast."

On an enjoyable sensory alert from her scent, he didn't wish to ponder his decision to take the Houston trip, but making Blythe happy seemed a good enough reason.

And deep down, he felt obliged to do something for Shelly, in light of having done nothing. How well he knew the dangers of marrying the wrong person.

Mostly, though, it had a gladdening effect, being closed up in a red Porsche with a redhead as flashy as her automobile. She pulled under Fill-Er-Fast's canopy; he didn't particularly want to pump gas in daylight, but only a jerk wouldn't offer. "I'll fill the tank. You get the map."

"Shall I see if they have sunglasses?"

"No."

"You could do with some new shades."

"Another casualty in Pomeranian versus Lord of the Castle." He readjusted the mangled wires that bit his nose. "Nippy's got an unhealthy disrespect for my property. Glad I didn't end up dog-sitting."

It seemed as if she was going to say something, but she didn't. In the bright of day Blythe went inside. Tom unfolded his hide from the car, and pulled his straw Stetson low on his brow and shoved the nozzle into the Porsche's tank.

A clutch of teenagers lolled against the convenience store wall. Just another summer day with nothing to do for those boys. What the youth of China Grove did with their time might be none of his concern, yet Tom couldn't stop thinking. Those boys ought to have something better to do with their time. Grandpa Rogers used to say, "Idle hands are the devil's workshop."

Too true.

"Ready?" Blythe asked, approaching the car.

"You bet. How about I drive?"

She shook her head. "A Porsche doesn't handle like a pickup. I'm used to it. I'll do the driving."

"You think I'm not up to a Porsche? Or is it that you think I can't be trusted with your dead husband's legacy?"

Ducking into the car, she shoved the key into the ignition and barked, "Get in. Now."

Tom did.

Her eyes went to his, as she said, "I'll be honest. I wouldn't be able to afford this car, if not for Jean-Pierre. I don't work for money. I work for the satisfaction of it. If you've got a problem with that, get out."

"I'm not getting out."

A long moment went by. Blythe arranged her handbag beneath the seat. She fidgeted. Her shoulders shifted. After she'd cleared her throat, she said, "Before we leave, I want to set the ground rules. No sex therapy."

"I wasn't planning any," he replied honestly. If he did get something going with Blythe, it wouldn't be clinical. What if they did? It would have to be mutually agreeable. And definitely in the dark of night.

The very dark of night.

Blythe eased the sports car onto the feeder road to the interstate. Once they were doing seventy on IH-10, going eastbound, she said out of the blue, "You know, you were right when you said we'd do well not to talk about the relationships we've had since...our parting. Wise words."

"I thought we were talking about a Porsche." Tom crossed his arms and eyed the unremarkable terrain. He waxed philosophical. "You know, sweet'eart. It's funny, the things we expect from life. They hurt us. Best we not expect anything from each other, then we'll do okay, until it's time for us to say *adios.*"

"Don't expect anything? Sounds like a plan."

From her profile, he got the impression she'd be happy if he never again brought up the subject of his regained virility. Strange. Blythe had been a passionate girl, and he suspected the woman was even more passionate. Strange, all right, the amalgam of the girl of yesterday and the woman of today. He just couldn't fit the piece in the puzzle, Blythe's being cold.

Or was it all an act?

Act or not, he was hurt. "Forget what I said about

driving your car. Hell, I'm not a Porsche man. What I need, though, is a better attitude."

"I'll buy that."

"You need restaurants. We need time away from China Grove. I can do restaurants." *I suppose.* "You'll notice, I hope, that I am willing to take a chance with flashing dashes."

"I noticed."

Nothing more got said, and again he studied the mundane. Hereabouts, the ho-hum of occasional trees and livestock dotted open vistas; the sky threatened to burst. Well, studying the sky beat trying to come up with something profound to say.

When they had reached midway through the two-hundred-mile trip between Sweet Creek Ranch and the missing teenagers, Tom ventured to say, "Is the idea of our making love repulsive?"

"Of course not."

Then why did she hesitate? Better put, what was she looking for? *Think, Tillman.* When they had parted as kids, she'd been expecting marriage. Now she was widowed. He was divorced. She might be wanting strings. "You looking to get married, Redd?"

"No!"

"Whew. You had me worried there for a minute."

Dumb thing to admit, that. She glared at him. Too bad there weren't any of those quick-learning centers where men could figure out how to second-guess women.

What he needed to do was lighten up.

"How 'bout flipping on the air conditioner?" he asked. "I'm hot."

"Sorry. Wasn't thinking." She got cool air to swirl. "I never overheat. I'm acclimated."

"No joke. Superhuman Generalissima Redd. But that's a switch, never heating up. I remember a girl, well, it didn't take much to find her hot spots."

That girl's behind shifted on the bucket seat. "Really, Tom, you do need to do something about those shades."

So much for heat. "If you'll stop at one of those stores at the western edge of Houston, you could go inside and pick me out a new pair. Fang-proof."

He charged forward with another tease. "Let's back up to other people's property. It took guts to pour my aftershave down the john."

She flashed a naughty grin before returning her focus to the road.

"Say, didn't you mention replacing my grievous loss? Stop by the aftershave counter while you're in the store, will you?" He edged toward her. "I do want to smell good to you," he said truthfully. "Like you do to me."

She fidgeted again. "Shades and splash it is. If you'll promise not to budge, in case the car phone rings."

"You've got a deal."

A few moments passed, Coastal Plains whizzing by. "Looks like we're driving into bad weather. Too bad we're not making this trip for an Astros game," she said wistfully. "I rarely get to watch real baseball, and we wouldn't have to worry about wetting our tootsies in the Astrodome. I miss baseball."

"That's your reward for taking up with berets and Partners in Crisis. Tell me something, Redd. Do Frenchmen eat quiche?"

Challenging to the nth degree, she darted him another

quick look, saying, "Why don't you book a seat on Air France and find out for yourself?"

"No thanks." Tom fingered his hat brim. "What was he like, your Frenchman?" Did he really want to know this?

"Époustouflant."

That weird word garbled in Tom's ears. It didn't bear much resemblance to the Texas language. The most he could make of her word, if he put a local translation to it? "You hooked up with a pussyfooter?"

"You know, Tom, sometimes you're a marvel." She chuckled. "But, no, Jean-Pierre wasn't a pussyfooter. He was great."

"I knew I didn't want to hear this."

"You're fairly *époustouflant,* feeling bad about Shelly and wanting to find her. Exercising, and getting out of the house."

"Call me Mr. Wonderful."

She chewed her bottom lip, sighed, then announced, "I'd like to know more about your wondrous deeds. Wait, hold the plane. I'm waiting until you're ready."

"Good."

"I'm hoping you'll open up on this trip."

"Could happen." Needing a switch of subjects, he thought back on one of her Texas brags. "How's it going with your campaign to get Granny Myrt in an Oliver Rockford movie?"

"Excellent."

"You don't say. You squirmed last night when she asked about him."

"I haven't contacted him. Yet." Another squirm. "I will."

"You're fidgeting like you're about to wet your britches."

"Why don't you just *fermez la bouche,* and open that Houston map! We need to find our way to the Aztec."

Tom didn't know anything about fermented bushes, but it got expressed like "shut up." Sounded kinder than shut up, though. He opened the map. "Motel's on the east side, near the Ship Channel. Stinks around there. Refinery breath."

"Not a very good part of town apparently."

"Glad I brought Granny Myrt's bazooka, is all I can say."

"You didn't." Horror-stricken, Blythe clutched the wheel tightly, like the bottom rung of a helicopter ladder. "No guns, Tom. I hate them."

"Strange. Your world turns on guns."

"That's why I hate them. I see what they do to people."

Tom had never taken a bullet. He didn't want Blythe to take one, either. He could rant, could rave, could yell, but he saw the futility in those. She would rant, rave and yell right back.

The only course to take? Supposed indifference. Tom took a pen to the map and started drawing a line from the interstate, charting their route to the motel. "Mmm, yeah. Well. Whatever."

"I don't think I've ever stopped here," she said, drawing his attention momentarily to the Schulenburg exit sign. "Is this a county seat by any chance?"

"No. Seat's in LaGrange."

"I love old courthouses. Looking one over would

break up the trip. I'm sure it'll do you good to stretch your legs.''

"Mmm." The machinations of getting to the Aztec without having to draw Granny Myrt's bazooka would do him better.

Blythe was saying something.

"Tom Tillman, must I ask twice? Will we, or will we not, pass a county seat between here and Houston?''

"Next town. Columbus." Glancing quickly at storm clouds, he drew an alternate route on the map, feeling better for it. "Columbus is a county seat.''

He refolded the map and tried to blank his mind of Blythe getting shot. He settled the bazooka between his legs. Somehow he nodded off. He awoke to a car door slamming closed; the engine wasn't running. He recognized the town square of Columbus. She'd parked in a slot, in front of the clapboard office of the Texas Department of Public Safety.

"What's going on?" he asked, an emptiness between his legs.

"The sheriff's office moved to the highway, so I settled for the state troopers. I've entrusted Myrtle's Beretta to them.''

"What? Why?''

"We're going to leave it here. We'll pick up Myrtle's gun on the return trip, provided you have a license to carry it.''

"Are you nuts? I'm not leaving my grandmother's piece with some do-right boy." Anyhow, Tom didn't have a license. What the hell would he have needed a license for before now? "I brought it along to protect you.''

She darted a glance at Tom, started the car and eased

out of the parking space. "Protection like that, I won't have."

He got a bad feeling, and was justified in it, when she admitted, "I've seen bullets tear people apart. Homes blown away. Families left in dire straits. And..." She gave too ardent attention to the road. "I've been shot myself, Tom."

Shot.

He felt as if he'd taken a bullet.

He turned up his collar, nudged the shades up the bridge of his snout and notched the hat down over his forehead. Settled in for a long summer's sulk. But thought better about that. "You owe me one. A big one. That was an expensive equalizer," he said to get his mind off the image of Blythe shot. The world wouldn't be a better place without Blythe; *he* wouldn't be a better person—or a better man—without her.

"Really, Tom, you're making too much of it."

"Just ferment your bush."

"What?"

"Forget it. Drive, woman!"

Sheets of rain tumbled. German-engineered windshield wipers dispensed with the sheets. The Porsche kept up with the rainstorm's fury as no broken-down pickup of a man could against the rainstorm of worry.

Like his pickup, he hadn't had his blades changed in years.

He was just an old rusted truck, not even able to protect his Redd against trouble. Damn. "Say your prayers, pussycat, we won't need that bazooka."

He prayed he'd get over his feelings of inadequacy where Blythe was concerned. More than anything, he wanted to be her hero.

Chapter Eight

"See. Everything's fine." Blythe nodded an "I told you so" once she'd finished telephoning Margaret, after she and Tom were ensconced in a second-level room at the Aztec Motel, much later than a two-hundred-mile trip should have taken. Cheerily, she added, "You worried for nothing."

"Don't gloat." Tom's scowl threatened to freeze his face, so long had he held it. He shook rain from bags emblazoned *Foley's* and tossed them above her duffel bag, atop the pasteboard dresser. Scanning their quarters, he said, "What a dump."

"Look on the sunny side. It's nice and dry." Dry, yes. But it smelled slightly of mildew and the cheesy aroma of former occupants. Blythe opened a window. Closed it quickly. The sulfurous odor of refineries had added to the stench. Anyway, Tom's expensive new aftershave, a delightful woodsy scent, mustn't be overpowered. "Our stay won't be awful."

He tossed his rain-splattered hat aside and ran fingers through his hair, where the hatband had mashed it. "It's not over yet."

Indeed. But like she'd said, they had arrived without bodily harm.

Picking their way through the monsoon, they had experienced quite a ride into the seedy part of the city. Located near the Port of Houston, the Aztec—Cash Only, No Credat Cards!—appealed to a certain run of clientele. She'd seen the type on distant wharfs. Rough. This was no place for teenagers. Especially not with night falling on a storm.

Icky and Shelly, as it were, weren't in quarters.

Yesterday the rapper hopeful had been met by a skinny girl with wild black hair, according to the room clerk, a man of Arabic extraction with a much-too-familiar-sounding name. Information hadn't come cheap. A brace of twenties in addition to the room rent had gone from Tom's wallet to the palm of Saddam Hussein. Thereafter, the room clerk had been more than pleased to present the key to the room next to Icky's.

Icky's quarters being located at the far end of the Aztec's upper walkway, the kids had to pass by on their way to their own accommodations. Blythe and Tom would wait here for them.

She wanted to search the big city more overtly, but recognized the futility of such a search. She grabbed her duffel. "Think I'll change into dry clothes."

Tom eyed her car keys. "I hope that extra forty bucks is enough for Hussein to do his job."

The room clerk, for an extra brace of twenties, had agreed to make certain her car didn't get stolen. "One can only hope."

Whatever the case, Blythe and Tom were secreted in a room with a faded red bedspread covering the king-size bed. Too bad Icky's room hadn't adjoined one with a pair of beds. Perhaps in Paris's elegant Hotel Georges Cinq.

"Tom, aren't you going to change?" Blythe asked, worried his clothes were as sodden as hers.

"No need. I had my hat and our bags as a raincoat. Only thing wet about me is the damper you've put on the trip."

"Give it a rest." She folded the bedspread to place it in a far corner. "Would you mind checking the linens for bedbugs?"

A sour expression on his face, Tom did. "Sheets're clean."

"Good." Blythe took her duffel to the bathroom and began to unpack toiletries. She never allowed herself to travel with many sundry items, not even makeup. Too many luxuries had a way of spoiling her; she couldn't allow herself to get spoiled. Nevertheless, she'd tucked away a bottle of Essence Douze. One small luxury never hurt.

She shrugged into fresh garments, and amended her count. She'd also included her silk nightie—her only nightie that had made it to Texas with her. How dumb, letting an opportunity go by at Foley's. She mumbled, "I should've bought a granny gown." Where was the nightgown? "Isn't this the pits?"

"You say something?" Tom asked in a peevish voice.

"I forgot my nightie."

"Oh, ho! Solid planning makes for success," he called into the bathroom, echoing her words of some time back.

At least his tone had improved.

"I'm usually an ace with packing," she said, rifling through the duffel, just to make sure.

"Freud at work here, Redd?"

"No, Freud is *not* at work here. I simply forgot it."

Too bad she couldn't forget her growling stomach. It had been hours on end since breakfast. Fried chicken and a nice dessert would hit the spot. "Are you hungry?"

"For what?"

"Food." She exited the bathroom. And gasped.

He was tugging his shirttail from jeans. Distracted from visions of sugarplums and chicken legs, she muttered, "No telling how long this stakeout will last."

A crack of thunder shook the window, punctuating her grouse.

He slouched into the room's one chair; his arms folded behind his head, he gazed at her. His teasing manner returned. "So...Ms. Perfect Packer, what would you like to do, besides chowing down, while we wait for Shelly?"

"I can't sit still. It gives me the fidgets."

"Those again? Want me to check your britches for ants?"

"In your dreams." Yet her urges roared, *Go for it!*

"The night's young. Lots of time for dreaming."

He picked up the channel changer that sat conveniently beside his chair, and went about his favorite occupation. Images flashed on the TV screen, of a man and a woman getting to know each other in the Old Testament sense.

"Man alive," he murmured, crouching his upper body toward the images. "Would you look at that?"

"Turn it off." Blythe parked her backside at the head of the bed. "We're not here to feed your prurient appetites."

The screen blackened. Reaching for the phone, he got the room clerk on the line. "Hussein, Tillman here. Room two-twelve. Yeah, yeah. I know. We've been watching it. It's roused a powerful appetite in my woman—"

He got a pillow to the head for that remark.

"We're hungry," he amended. "There's another forty bucks in it if you'll run a few errands. You will? Good. That's what I like, cooperation."

"Who's going to watch my car?" she asked, her question ignored.

"Pizza's good there? Sounds fine. Order a big one, everything on it. We'll want Big Reds and root beers, too. And ice. Pick up a six-pack of beer while you're at it. None of that imported stuff. How about air freshener? This room smells like hell. I know, I know. That's the Ship Channel for you."

"What jolly chatter," she muttered.

"Oh, Hussein…" Tom winked at her. "See what you can do about finding a bouquet of white roses and a few candles."

Blythe fumed. Bringing him along had indeed asked for trouble. Obviously he figured to turn this rescue mission into a romantic idyll. He confirmed her suspicions by swiveling to the side, hunching a shoulder over the mouthpiece and whispering, "Yeah, sure. Okay. Add some of those. Uh, um…" His voice lowered even more. "Large."

"What élan," she said, once he and his cohort had finished the shopping list.

"Does that mean dash or flash?"

"Basically." Her lips tightened. "Let's speak hypothetically. Let's assume I get hot to go the Nightingale route. Let's assume you'll want to bare your butt to those candles you've ordered, and my eyes. Let's—"

"I'd be willing to give it a try. In the dark."

"You would. But you also promised we wouldn't get into sex therapy."

His grin was both infuriating and evocative. "Therapy never entered my mind."

Not to be put off, Blythe continued. "Let's assume Shelly and Icky show up. Would they hear anything as they walk by? Since you can't go three minutes on Diablo, how fast could we make ourselves presenta—"

"I can go three minutes. No. Four."

She studied the grin that lifted his sexy mouth, a smile loaded with innuendo. "Wow, Tom. I'm impressed. With stamina such as yours, you could go for the gold at the sexual Olympics."

His face fell. "Guess you're right."

Uh-oh. Bad thing, bringing up his inadequacies. Yet each time she'd challenged him, he'd risen to the occasion. Sheesh. He even turned her thoughts to double entendres. "I'm sure you'll do fine, when the time comes. When you get a *willing partner*."

"Willing? I don't like the sound of that." His fingers

inched between the shirt snaps to scratch his chest. "Sounds like you'd never give me a chance to be…my old self."

"Give it up. Now."

He exhaled heavily through his nose and sat back in the chair, staring at the blank TV set. After a lapse in moments, he said, "How bad was that gunshot wound?"

"I survived," she hedged.

"Guess that counts for something." In an obvious change of tactics, since he apparently sensed that castigating her would do nothing but set her off, he shoved up from his seat. "You know, I haven't done a push-up since the fire. With Diablo hitched to the porch back home, I ought to do something to keep up my cardios."

Was she ever glad he hadn't changed the subject.

"Think I'll do push-ups."

"Not too many," she cautioned, but she was pleased he'd accepted the gauntlet. "You're not ready for too many."

"Let *me* decide when I'm ready for *what*."

He swung to the floor, flipped to his stomach and braced for push-ups. She swallowed. He might not put bodybuilders to shame, but he looked darned good. His body a long, lean line, his muscles straining and showing off tight buns, his teeth bared to the throes of exertion— oh, my! The blatant voyeurism of watching what could be considered Tom in the act, appealed to Blythe. She'd never been a voyeur. But she couldn't tear her eyes from him. Her insides stirred. Her veins pulsed with warming blood. Well, Terrific Tom had always elicited things best ignored.

Unless Shelly and Icky showed up soon, this would become a very, very long stakeout.

By the time Hussein dropped off the soggy bounty—a good two hours after he'd taken Tom's order—Blythe found herself ravenous to the max. The food tasted good, too.

They were too famished to light the candles. Before he plunged into the pizza box, though, Tom did spray the room. He also cleared the channel changer away to place the vase of white roses on the bedside table.

"White is your favorite," he commented, rightly.

She and Tom occupied the bed, with him braced against the headboard and her sitting Indian-style at the foot of it. They dug into the pizza as if it were the last supper. She chugged a soda; he had two or three beers before lighting the candles and snuffing the lamp.

Ah, candlelight...not bad. Good, in fact. Even the Aztec held a certain élan.

Eyelids heavy, Tom gazed at her. "You look beautiful in candlelight," he whispered, the ambience even more pleasant.

"You're not hard on the eye, either." She decided he'd put on a pound or two lately. His shoulders nice and wide, his hair brushed them in a kempt fashion. Her gaze slipped down the length of him, passing by his opened shirt and catching on the button he'd loosened at the top of his jeans. Her eyes locked on the hillock beneath the snaps. *You're still a hunk.*

This air-conditioned room suddenly turned quite warm.

"Think I'll lower the thermostat," she said. "I'm hot."

"Thought you didn't get—never mind." He winked. "Is it too warm for a massage? I brought the oils. Hint, hint. You know, you do owe me for Granny Myrt's bazooka."

"Call Hussein. I'll bet for another forty bucks, he'd rub your back himself."

"Okay. Massage's out. What're we gonna do, sweet'eart? We're both hot. We're alone together." He grinned wickedly. "And…I forgot my nightie, too."

"Sleep in our clothes."

"I'm not the big bad wolf."

He slid his ankle against her knee, as if she weren't already very aware of his presence, wasn't already undergoing overheated senses and sensual longings.

"I'm Tom," he murmured. "The guy who loved you, from the time you were fifteen."

"Somewhere behind baseball and ranching and a little number named Dana. You're the yo-yo who called my car my best feature."

"If I've made you bitter, I'm sorry."

"Don't flatter yourself," Blythe flung back, fearing he'd struck the truth. Was she bitter?

She grappled to settle on their reason for being here. "Wonder what's happened to Icky and Shelly."

"Could be they're married. Could be they're doing what we did, when we were their age. Exploring, discovering, being so in love that it hurts."

"I wouldn't wish first love on anyone."

He cocked his head, his brow grooving. "You are bitter."

Her repressed feelings opened like a book. "You fried my heart, Tom."

"That bad? I can attest to how burns hurt." He twisted forward, going up on his knees to meet her. His woodsy scent got to her, or was it his next words? "I'm sorry, Redd. I'm sorry for everything. Especially for not standing in the way of your getting on that plane for Germany."

A broad fingertip traced her jaw, her earlobe; he started to press his lips to hers. "Forgive me."

She didn't accept his kiss. "I...I don't want to talk about Germany."

"Okay. But I want you to know, I've decided I got burned as punishment. My just deserts for letting go the best thing that ever happened to me. You. Give me another chance, precious one. We've done enough hurting."

"Amen to that."

"Amen to that," he echoed. "I'd like to make it up to you."

She smiled.

Assuaged by tender words and soft pleas, she allowed him to guide her to her back, crossways on the bed. He settled beside her. One arm slid beneath her neck, to cradle her to him. The other hand, the one that had been injured, canvassed her shoulder, her arm, her wrist.

She snuggled closer. All sorts of spots tightened in her insides—marvelous tingles and contractions. He felt even better to her than he had as a teenager.

The Aztec suddenly seemed as lavish as the Georges Cinq.

"You're crying." He kissed her moist cheek, taking

her tears onto his tongue. "I promise you, you'll never shed another tear over me. Forever. For always."

Even if he meant his promises, this had to stop. He talked like a man in love. Once, he'd professed his love. But where had that gotten them? Why hadn't she thought of that *before* leaving Florida?

"Are those footsteps I hear?" she asked, knowing full well they weren't.

Tom unwound his arms and settled back, the mood broken, as she'd intended. "Guess you'd better check it out," he said. "Since it's plain you're not interested in any reunion beyond the high-school thing."

"You know me too well."

"No, Redd. I wish I did know you."

Not doing a good job of it, Tom worked on lowering his libido by thinking inane thoughts; Blythe left the bed to switch the air conditioner off.

"If the kids pass us," she said, unlatching the window, "I'll wake up if this is open. Besides, there's a nice breeze."

Funny, how she could crab about Balkan Breeze, then opt for the reek of what smelled like a sulphur match. So be it. He'd gotten the picture, even before she found an excuse to avoid intimacy. She just didn't want him. All right, he'd pushed her. He could back off. Might be best. While his arousal had returned, he didn't feel too confident about waltzing around naked.

After dousing the candles, he shucked all but his briefs, slid between the sheets and kept to the bed's edge. "Good night," he said, forcing an even tone and closing his eyes.

Sleep, he didn't. He knew when Blythe stripped to panties and bra, knew when she got into bed. He sensed her, smelled her. He wanted her. He'd never been more awake.

Within minutes he heard her breathing turn to that of sleep. He clutched the headboard as if it were one of her ladders. It didn't help, listening to rain. Rain was the best time for lovemaking. He'd never forgotten the one time they had been stranded in the barn, rain pouring...

He counted sheep. He counted to a hundred, forward and backward. He counted the times Blythe had mountain-climbed his porch, remembering how she'd looked. And how she moved in different moods. He felt the bed shift. She'd flipped over. Was nestled against his back, murmuring as if she'd found something pleasant.

"Redd," he said in a voice loud enough to wake her. She didn't budge. If anything, she nestled closer. "Redd," he repeated to no avail. "What's this about noise waking you?" Nothing. "I hear the kids," he shouted.

Again, nothing. She was out.

He rolled over and drew her to him. "Wake up, dammit."

"You say something?" she asked drowsily.

"I said, wake up."

"I'm awake."

"Good."

Her arm snaked around his neck, drawing him closer. "Nice."

If that wasn't a dark-of-night invitation, what was? He touched, explored, caressed her face and arms. He hadn't lost his touch with bra snaps. Soon, her breasts overfilled his hands, then his mouth. Their passions were building to a fevered pitch, and he felt wholly capable of fulfilling her every desire.

"Oh, so nice," she murmured again.

He touched her as he once had. Touched her as he'd fantasized about doing, more times than he should have. Her arms and legs felt like soft satin. She was warm, so warm. Neither memory nor fantasy had ever been fine as reality.

Light-headed, he ached to free her of her French-cut panties. He tried. The moment he'd worked them over her hips and his fingers had cupped her backside, she whispered, "You make me feel so good."

He wanted her. Here. In the dark. As if nothing stood between making love and the nebulous future.

The future.

Whoa.

She had her ideals that he didn't fit. Hell, he didn't think he ever could. He decided to cool his libido with a worst-thought scenario. Where on her abdomen was her scar? Bang. He heard the gunshot, knew it came from his thoughts.

He shot from bed. "Go back to sleep."

"Why?"

"Because I said!"

"Did you... Tom, if you're worried about your performance, don't."

"Just ferment your bush, Redd."

"I swear, I'll never understand you."

"That makes two of us."

He shrugged into his clothes, necessarily posting himself in the chair. He gazed across the darkened room, barely making out Blythe's form, yet his mind's eye pictured her, clear as glass. Big, beautiful, brave. Always ready for a challenge, or to give one. She could take a bullet and go on with her life.

He'd gotten burned, and couldn't see the light of day.

He knew what he needed to do. He had to make the transformation Blythe kept suggesting. It wouldn't be easy. He didn't know if he was up to it, but he could try. Would try.

Two in the morning. Tom grabbed the room key, his hat and wallet. He made sure to tuck the cover beneath Blythe's chin before locking the door behind him. He legged it to the Aztec's office. Hussein wasn't on duty, hadn't been for hours. Not good.

Worse, the night clerk, a pleasant woman named Riccarla, went the pity route once she got a gander at Tom. "You poor man," she said, a Plexiglas barrier between them. "You've suffered a hideous accident, haven't you?"

He almost bolted. "No, I was born this way," he answered, determined not to accept pity nor to bolt. "Listen, I need change for the pay phone. And a phone book. Can you help me?"

She did.

He called the police and hospitals; his efforts turned up nothing on Icky and Shelly's whereabouts. *No news is good news.* Then he went behind the Aztec to check on Blythe's Porsche.

Once he saw it, he groaned. How was he going to explain *this?* Damn. What were they going to do now?

* * *

Blythe awoke in the Aztec to an incessantly ringing telephone, no rain…and no Tom. Where was he? The clock read three in the morning. She took care of the most pressing matter. The phone.

"This is Margaret," the caller said, a tear in her voice.

The news wasn't terrible, but it wasn't good, either.

Concerned and worried, Blythe shivered.

Where was Tom when she needed him?

As soon as she rang off, she jumped from bed and rushed into the shower. Where was Tom?

She dried off, dressed. Ran the toothbrush around her teeth, and fingers through her hair. Found her sandals and ear hoops. The clock read 4:00 a.m. Where was Tom?

And why, after the many crises she'd faced alone, did she suddenly have a need for anyone?

The instant she decided to leave the room, either to look for him or to leave a note if he couldn't be found, he unlocked the motel room door and stepped inside. His hat rode extra low on his brow.

Glad to see him, angry at his absence, she rushed forward, placing her hands on his shoulders. "Where have you been?"

"Making, um… Walking around, mostly. Did some calling earlier, to see if I could get word on Shelly and her suitor."

"I've gotten word. They were in a car accident, leaving a rap concert."

Tom paled. "Are they…all right?"

"Too early to tell. They're at the hospital. I told Margaret we'd go to them. She's already on her way. Let's go."

"Damn. Double damn. This is all my fault. I should've listened to Shelly about the marriage bit." Tom groaned. "Are they married?"

"All Margaret knew was they wrecked on Navigation Boulevard. Probably on their way back here."

Tom rubbed his neck. "This is all my fault."

"Forget hindsight. And what would it serve, anyway? I told Margaret we'd go to the hospital. It's over in the Medical Center, south of downtown Houston. She'll meet us there."

"What about Icky's mom?"

"I haven't the slightest idea. Let's go," she repeated.

"We've got a problem. Another problem." He swiveled around to face her. "Someone stole the tires off your car."

Shocked and disgusted, Blythe gritted her teeth and parked fists on her hips. "So much for the protective powers of your buddy Hussein."

"Hey, I made a mistake. I make them. Get over it."

"I'm not used to being pushed around."

"I'm not used to being away from home. But here we are, in a seedy motel in a strange town, those kids in a fix. So smooth your feathers, woman, and listen up. I've arranged for a wrecker to dolly your car to a tire shop. This is Sunday—the place won't open till noon. Riccarla, the night clerk, offered to rent me her Oldsmobile. I've rented it. Now…do you want to stand here arguing? Or do you want to go to the hospital?"

Blythe would be staked naked to the bald rims of her car before she'd compliment him on his organizational skills. "I don't want to hear one more word out of you about 'owing one.'"

"Whatever you say." A grin shoved up his face. "Dearest."

Dearest? Nice ring to that.

Tom started to grab their belongings, but straightened to eye her. His grin gyrated to what might be considered seriousness. "Would any of this qualify as flash or dash?"

What could Blythe do but laugh with genuine affection?

Blythe was proud of Tom. He might have turned his collar up and hidden his face below that Stetson before entering the bright lights of the emergency room, but he had taken another step toward facing the world.

They found Shelly, her eye blackened, sitting in a quiet corner of the waiting area. Blythe decided the eye pretty much matched the girl's disheveled state.

"I'm cool," she said immediately. "Icky will be, too. The docs are X-raying him, just to make sure nothing's broken."

"You and Icky could've saved yourself a trailerload of pain," Tom observed, swiveling into the seat next to the girl, "if you'd stayed home."

Blythe went to the coffeepot, filled foam cups and handed them over. She noticed the girl's fingers trembling.

Shelly's lip did more than tremble. "To tell the truth, nothing's cool. Everything's turned out cruddy. Our plans, everything!"

Blythe smoothed the teenager's wild black hair. "Shelly, dear, did you and Icky get married?"

"That's a laugh. The courthouse clerk didn't buy into our fake birth certificates."

Empathy rife, Blythe couldn't even feel relieved at the foiled wedding. Thwarted first love. Hard on the heart, that. She glanced at Tom, remembering the old feelings, the old insecurities, the old aches and pains. And the joy and euphoria of simply being in love.

She'd been wrong. Everyone should know the pleasure of it.

Tears burst. "I need my mom! Where is she?"

"On her way," Tom answered. "Don't worry, Shelly. We're here for you."

A familiar thin woman with prominent teeth rushed into the waiting room, Nippy's head poking from her handbag. Margaret had arrived in record time. Shelly's adoptive mother raveled at the edges, worrying over her daughter and what had driven her to run from home.

At that moment Nippy growled. Icky walked into the waiting room. Without his usual swagger. His Born to Raiz Hell arm was in a sling. "Been released," he said abruptly.

Margaret stomped to him. "I want you to stay away from my daughter."

"Mom," Shelly wailed like the prairie wind.

Looking down at the sling on his arm, then up at Shelly, Icky said, "Shelly, I gotta blow this town."

Blythe's heart thunked for Shelly.

Balled fists had gone to Shelly's face. "No, Icky. No."

"Feel the heat. Gotta retreat."

"Before you do." Tom stepped up to him, held out his palm. "I understand you have your mother's credit cards and money. I'll be happy to give them back to her for you.''

"Uh, yeah. Those. Um, thanks, man. Could you help get 'em outta my wallet?'' He lifted his sling slightly.

The moment Tom had retrieved Mrs. Kuleska's property, Icky's gaze soldered to Shelly's. "'Bye, chick. It was almost fun.''

He sauntered out of the waiting room.

"Icky!''

A pall draped the room. Margaret clamped her daughter's arm, keeping her from fleeing, saying, "Let him go.''

Shelly turned into her mom's arms. ''Take me home.''

Blythe remembered the hurt of first, failed love. Poor Shelly. Poor everyone who had ever lost out.

After Margaret had led Shelly from the hospital, Tom gently took Blythe's arm to walk toward their rental car. He thought about Shelly. Icky the creep had made an exit scene much too easily. Tom had seen in Shelly's eyes the ache of having a loved one walk away. He knew that pain. How would Shelly take it, in the long run? Would she turn to another boy, and make an even bigger mistake?

Couldn't make much more of a mistake than Icky Kuleska, though.

Near Riccarla's ancient Oldsmobile, Blythe said, "The tire store will open at noon. Should we try to find some breakfast?''

Breakfast? Tom ached to escape to China Grove. Feeling weary beyond his years from a lost night of sleep and the worries of other people's business, not to mention the situation with Blythe, he said, "Sure. Why not?"

That parting scene in the hospital had him troubled more than it ought to. He felt a powerful need to help restless teenagers. How, he had no idea.

He had a sudden thought. "Breakfast first, then why don't we rent a room at a swank hotel? After a power nap, we could make an evening of it at some swankier restaurant."

"Separate rooms."

"A suite." Tom tickled her earlobe, then opened the passenger door. "You wait here. I'll go use the pay phone to check with the Bentley Hotel. It's the best in town."

"This is probably not one of my better decisions," Blythe murmured and slid inside the old Rocket 88.

Chapter Nine

The management of the Bentley Hotel took one look at the scarred, sleep-deprived, ponytailed cowboy in rumpled clothes and claimed a mistake had been made. The reservation clerk wouldn't even suggest a place for breakfast. He did suggest Tom try the ten-dollar motel on the edge of town.

Glad Blythe had stayed in the car, Tom had the urge to grab the guy's throat, but he tipped his hat instead. "Thank you, sir. That's mighty kind of you. I'll remember your kindness."

He used the pay phone in the lobby to call every nice hotel in town. No luck. He ached to be back at the ranch, within the familiarity of his own little world. This transformation business was hell.

"We may have to settle for another motel," he told

Blythe once he reached the Oldsmobile. "Not a seedy one, though. I draw the line there."

For the longest time after leaving the Bentley, Blythe drove the elderly 88 down South Main and over Old Spanish Trail, then up Travis and alongside Holcombe. Tom's eyes combed the plethora of posted No Vacancy signs at nicer motels. On the second go-round, just to make sure someone didn't hold out, his tired feet and less-than-solid ego did the legwork.

He needed rest. Wouldn't even mind cuddling up with fox-colored fur, so long as he could lay down his weary head.

"Forget the room." He slid onto the seat for the umpteenth time. "Let's go home. To the ranch. I'll buy you a waffle on the way out of town, at the Pancake House."

"Pessimist. We'll find a room. Wish we had my car."

"Yeah, yeah, yeah." The car wouldn't be ready until late afternoon, they had learned. "If we had your Porsche, we could do some phoning without leaving the comfort of leather seats. You should've bought one of those portable cell phones. Even I know those're the modern way to go." *Ease up.* "Redd, have a heart. I'm losing steam."

Blythe, on the other hand, looked full of steam.

"We could sit at the tire store. You could rest there."

There was no resting at the place, but they did retrieve Blythe's car by midafternoon. And a vending machine provided stale baked goods. Tom changed clothes in the men's room.

Once he'd called Riccarla and told her where to find the Oldsmobile, he and Blythe set out for another turn at finding accommodations. They took off in the Porsche.

"Let's give the Warshire Hotel a try," he ordered. "Now."

While Tom drew his hat down, Blythe wheeled her red charger under the porte cochere of the elegant hotel. A valet bowed and scraped, as did the doorman. As if by magic, the reservation clerk produced the key to a suite.

Tom decided he ought to look into buying a car capable of gaining entrance to such hallowed ground as the Warshire. He wasn't one for hallowed ground. Blythe was.

She fit right in. In Tom's eyes this woman had the look of fine hotels and finer champagne. She *deserved* the look and someone who could provide it.

"Yummy. Isn't this place divine?"

"Sorta seems sterile to me," Tom replied.

She ignored his negativism.

Their two-bedroom suite with balcony had proven as tasteful as the reception area, a welcome discovery. Blythe was more than ready for a taste of luxury and a fine à la carte meal. But Tom looked in dire need of a nap. Well, he had been without sleep last night. "Take a nap," she suggested. "I'm going to phone Margaret. Make sure they got home all right."

"Good ideas. A shower sounds good, too. I'll hold off on the nap. Ring Margaret."

The Saldivars had indeed arrived home safely. Ed was there, too. Blythe wouldn't ask, but Margaret volunteered, "Shelly's okay, all things considered. She's sleeping."

Relating the news to Tom, Blythe worried about Shelly. And Icky. Maybe she saw too much of herself and Tom in those two.

Determined to shake the blues, she opened the sitting-dining room's balcony doors onto a view of Miller Park, finding something bland to say. "Too many times I've stayed in hotels where the lobby's okay, then the rooms are dreadful."

"Beats the ranch's world headquarters, I guess."

"Without a doubt. This hotel may not rank up there with the Georges Cinq in Paris, but they both hearken back to the elegance of bygone days. Dinner jackets, cupped trumpets, golden cigarette cases. Know what I mean?"

"I'm still new to this élan stuff." Tom yawned and pressed on toward one of the bedrooms. "Glad you aren't disappointed. Me, I need a shower and shut-eye. Order breakfast."

It was way past the hour to break one's fast.

Oh, well.

Not at all in need of sleep, Blythe rang room service and ordered a superb service of tea and its accompaniments. She examined the minibar and so forth. She buzzed with energy.

Tom slept.

She hankered for more. Exactly the extent of "more," she chose not to reflect on.

She watched a movie. A tear-jerker. Took a bath. On the off chance that Tom might wish to dine lavishly, she called the concierge and asked her to make early dinner reservations at a tony spot. Then she made a few turns on the balcony that overlooked Miller Park. A band began to play at the pavilion.

She read the TV schedule. Pined for a fresh manicure. She felt like a caged animal. Was Tom never going to wake up?

The hour for dinner reservations came and went.

She called Hollywood and left a recorded message at Oliver Rockford's production office, leaving the hotel number as well as the ranch's.

Afterward, she found cheese and crackers in the mini-bar, then rang Myrtle.

"Some feller in London phoned you," Myrtle said. "Earlier today. He said there's some nasty deal going on in Africa, and you need to be there."

Interest raced through Blythe's veins.

"Said his name was Marmalade. I think."

"Sir Montgomery Honeybone," Blythe corrected.

"That's it. He said for you to knock him up."

Blythe noted the time. Nine in the evening. Very early morning in London. Why panic? Often "situations" settled themselves. Tomorrow would be time enough for Partners in Crisis.

"Honey girl, what did he mean about knocking up? You ain't in the family way, are you?"

Blythe chuckled. "Sir Monty had a proper upbringing, but he uses slang. His was an English idiom for call him back."

"Whew, that's good to know," Myrtle replied. "I was scart there for a minute. Thought you had something weird going on."

"No. Just the everyday of a world health organization. And a lonesome evening in a hotel."

"Do they got room service and good-looking bell-hops?"

"Yes."

"Wish I was there," Myrtle said over the lines. "I'm bored as bored can be. I'm ready to spread my wings. Be sure that Rockford feller returns your call."

"I will. But don't give Sir Monty my number here at the hotel. I'll get in touch with him once I'm ready."

She rang off, but worried about not calling her superior. What if something awful had happened?

And how would Tom react to that Rockford call?

"Stop it," she warned herself.

Rockford, Africa and Sir Monty filed to the back of her mind, she decided this evening would be for Tom. She might have demanded no-holds, but what would it hurt? As long as she made certain not to get too ridiculous over him. First, though, he had to awaken.

Tom awoke disoriented in the strange surroundings of his room in the suite. He heard music from outside, from the park below. Damn. It was half past ten. He'd yet to make dinner arrangements. Was it too late to wine and dine?

Scrubbing his hand through his hair, he went to look for Blythe and found her napping in her room with the TV blaring.

He smiled. She looked so dear, lying there on her bed, her pillow plumped against her cheek. Dear Redd.

Damn their yesteryears. He hated that he'd hurt her, hated that she'd hurt him. Hated that life so often turned out lousy, not as it should be. Like with Shelly and Icky. Those two had been doomed from the start. Which was how people had looked at a pair of teenagers called Tom and Redd.

How would it turn out for them now?

"Our supper's here," he called. "Hope you don't mind eating at midnight."

Blythe set down her hairbrush and brushed her blouse with the heel of a hand. She smiled, wanting dinner and not in some restaurant. She wanted to be alone with Tom, here in the Warshire.

She stepped to the dining table, where room service had already laid out a rich meal. Woodsy-scented Tom helped her to a chair. At the table, facing him, she smiled with innumerable sentiments, most of the dizzying class.

What an indeed marvelous night for chateaubriand and Bordeaux wine. What a night for the dessert that waited nearby: a bottle of chilled French champagne, a plate of chocolate-dipped fruit. Apricots for her, strawberries for him.

A balmy night for the fanned-open balcony doors that allowed in the sounds of a big-band concert from Miller Park. "Green Eyes" played.

Tom had even ordered white roses.

Romance at its flashing height, this.

She gazed above a low-set candle at Tom, loving everything she saw. But she mustn't go on without explaining about her call to California.

"I tried to knock Oliver Rockford up."

Tom took an overlarge swallow of Bordeaux. When he quit coughing, he said, "You what? Isn't that kind of unusual, you being the woman?"

"I'm sure women do it to him all the time."

"Listen, sweet'eart, I know it's good not to have secrets, but it might be best to leave some things unsaid."

She winked. Cut a slice of beef. "It's not like that at all. I tried to phone him, as I promised Myrtle. Are you all right with that? It would be nice if she could have your blessing before she leaves."

"Give me a break. Just because you left a message doesn't mean he'll put my granny in pictures."

"True. But even if he's not interested, she should have her California adventure."

"She's old. Naive. No telling what would happen to her."

Blythe took another sip of wine. "She got by before you were born. She persevered while you were injured. She'll do fine on her own."

Tom toyed with his salad fork. "Yeah, you're right."

"It would be a nice gesture if you paid her way."

"She's got her own money. She doesn't need mine. I paid her a share when I parceled off the ranch. She talks big about wanting this and that, but she could buy herself the freedom she begs for, if she really wanted to."

"Not surprising, that news. She's adorable in a strange way. A true piece of work."

"Have to agree with your way of looking at my oddball granny. I guess the off-center appeals to me. I'm lucky to have her." His expression added, *I'll miss her.* "Matter of fact," he said, "I'm a lucky man, period. You came back."

"You know I'll be leaving."

Sadness flickered deeper in his features. "That's the rough part. I've gotten used to your ordering me around."

She stared at her plate.

"I don't know what I'll do, rattling around by my-self."

Blythe yearned to offer to stay at the ranch until he'd reconciled to being alone, but she couldn't. It could be that Sir Monty would call her away, even before the reunion.

"You could find something else to do," she suggested.

"Whoa. No way. Not one word about livestock or horses."

"Livestock isn't the only way to spend time."

"Well, I have been thinking about...,"

"About what?"

Candlelight flickering in his blue eyes, his wineglass shoved aside, his wide shoulders curving toward her, he grinned. "Shall we dance?"

"I Love You For Sentimental Reasons" floated outside the balcony.

"What about dinner?"

"Leave it. Dance with me."

She rose to his enclosing arms. Having lost none of his ability to move to music, he guided her across the floor. She melted against him, reveling in the feel of him, so solid where a man needed to be.

As they spun to an elevated note, he whispered against her ear, eliciting a shiver of delight, asking, "I wonder how many lovers suspect Deek Watson wrote those lyrics with them in mind? My big, beautiful, bright Blythe, I'm never lonely, whenever you are in sight."

A rush of emotion caused her eyes to burn with tears.

Too well she knew another stanza, about never parting. She felt awful for damning him to loneliness.

He danced her to the balcony, where a breeze and the melody entwined them. "I'd like to go home. Tonight."

Of the same sentiment, she nodded. Soon they would say goodbye, perhaps sooner than she wished, and she didn't want to chance having to bid farewells in a Houston hotel. She wanted to remember Tom with the creek as backdrop.

"I can be ready in five minutes."

It took ten, since Blythe boxed up the dessert and tucked the champagne in her duffel bag.

When they reached the ranch house, she yearned to invite him to her room, or invite herself to his, at least for dessert. She didn't. She wanted to, though.

"Looky here."

"That's quite a CD player."

"Ain't it? I bought two. One for me. One for you and Tom. Bought y'all some compact discs, too. Old-fogy music, like the two of you used to dance to, back when you was in high school."

"Myrtle, that's very kind. Thank you. But..." Blythe, who'd been sitting alone on the porch this late afternoon, took off her sunglasses. "I'm afraid I may be leaving, too. Perhaps before you leave."

Oliver Rockford had called before noon and agreed to a screen test, the second Monday from now. Myrtle would leave the Sunday beforehand, the Sunday after the reunion. Already Blythe had called a travel agent for tickets and accommodations for Myrtle; she'd decided that she should pay expenses, not Tom. In the hindsight of knowing she'd leave soon, she felt that to ask him to finance Myrtle's trip would add insult to his injury.

Maybe she simply needed something to assuage her own guilt. She'd returned Sir Monty's telephone call. She was needed in Africa. For the first time in her nursing life, she didn't hunger to fly off to duty.

"I'm thinking about asking Shelly to go with me." Myrtle set down the CD player and a plastic sack that obviously held compact discs, then took the chair next to Blythe. "She could stay a couple weeks, before school starts. We'll visit Mann's Chinese Theater, and eat at that hamburger place across the way, and go to Disneyland, and rollerblade on Venice Beach. I hear you can get tickets to TV shows, just for the asking."

"Have you talked to Margaret about it?"

"I have. She's of a mind for the trip. Shelly's moping around, driving her mama bananas. And now that Ed's home, he's been yammering about Shelly needing to get over Icky."

"I feel sorry for those kids," Blythe said. "It's not easy, giving up on first love."

Myrtle reached to squeeze her fingers. "I know that, honey girl. That's the reason I want to get li'l ol' Shelly away from here. So she won't think about that idiot what turned his back in Houston."

"Like I turned on Tom, even unintentionally?"

"You could look at it that way." A white brow jerked up.

Tom rounded the porch. He'd been at the stables for some reason, although Blythe entertained no thoughts that he'd been watering or feeding Pickles.

"I heard what you said, Granny Myrt. I don't think

getting Shelly's mind off Icky will work. She loves that boy. You might set her on a worse path, taking her to some strange place. Some strange and dangerous place.''

It went without saying that Tom remembered another young couple torn apart. So did Blythe.

Myrtle sighed. ''I'll keep an eye on her. I wasn't planning to take her to East L.A.''

He glanced down, then up at his grandmother. ''She needs something constructive and fun to do here in town.''

''Like what?'' Myrtle and Blythe said in unison.

''I don't know. I'm thinking on it.''

Myrtle took off for the pickup, saying, ''I'm going to town. Don't wait up for me. I'm going to show my boom box off to Prudence. You take this one and these CDs. Go do something with them, both of you.''

''We do need to talk,'' Blythe said to Tom.

He needed to know she was leaving. While she reached for the sack, he took the CD player. Together, they took off for the creek. Her first instinct was to stop him. The creek shouldn't be for bad news. Yet Blythe followed Tom.

He couldn't bring himself to look at her. He knew she sat on the creek bank next to Granny Myrt's purchase, knew Blythe hugged her knees while a slight breeze kicked at her soft curls. Tom fingered the compact discs, not wanting to hear any of these singers. Not wanting to be reminded of the past, needing to hold on to the present.

He still couldn't bring himself to look at her. He studied the trees, the water, the rocks, the grass. Everything but Blythe.

While he wanted to ask her opinion on an idea he had, he wouldn't. From the look on her face when he'd approached the porch, ideas didn't seem important. "You're leaving, aren't you?"

"Yes, Tom. I am. I need to be in London next Sunday. Partners in Crisis has a cargo plane going to Africa on Monday."

"A week from today."

Suddenly he needed music. To stop the sheer terror that was going through him, he needed something, even tunes to bring back memories. He shoved a disc into the player.

"Hoagy Carmichael."

"Yeah. 'Stardust.'" Finally he looked at her. She was clutching those knees as if her life depended on it. Maybe the music got to her, where he hadn't been able to. Maybe it was doing the same for him. "Remember that song? The band played it, the last hour of our junior prom. We decided it was our song. That our love would always be new. That we'd never be apart for long. That we'd share the music of the 'years gone by.'"

He stretched out on the grass, not trusting himself to take her hand, for fear he'd become a blubbering idiot, begging her to stay. It might be better if she did go away. Soon. Tom feared that if Blythe stayed much longer, he could never let her go, might do anything to stop her leaving.

"I don't want you to leave," Tom said in a hoarse whisper.

Blythe turned her head to study him. The sun an orange sphere to the west, bathing him in golden light, he was stretched out on the grassy bank, near enough to touch.

He asked too much. She stretched for the music machine and stuck another disc into it. "Stardust" had been too heady to take. Any more, and she feared a good reason not to leave would surface.

"The situation in Africa, it's not an uprising. It's famine," she said. "My team is going in with a relief effort. I won't be in danger."

"Oh, no. Of course not. No disease, no unrest. No hungry people going nuts and turning their hatred on the hands that feed them. Nah, never happen."

"You should look into a job as a professional worrier."

For a protracted moment he glared at her. "Maybe it's high time someone worried about you."

"I'm not used to being worried over."

"Don't you think you could get used to something new?"

All her adult life she'd charged forward, never fearing what might jump in front of her. She might not want it, but the idea of being cared for had its appeal. "Maybe I could. I don't know. I'm used to danger."

"There's an allure to it, I'll grant that. But, Redd, danger, well, it's dangerous. You've gotten a battle souvenir. You know they hurt. I know they hurt. I wish...I wish you could have saved me from diving into that fire."

She stilled, knowing full well he'd never before brought up the subject of the fire. Everything fell away but the hunger to hear what ticked in his heart, what had taken away the old Tom.

Hoping he'd open up, she asked, "Do you... Do you ever regret going in for those little girls?"

"Not for the Cherino sisters." He closed his eyes. "Ammanda and Julia were little, alone. Their mother had gone back to Mexico. Berto isn't much of a parent, either."

Between songs, silence fell. She heard nothing but the rushing water. And his ragged breathing.

"What happened in the fire, Tom? I'd like to know."

With a slight nod rife with contemplation that, she supposed, tried to masquerade as nonchalance, he said, "The girls' father owed me money. He'd worked for a while at the ranch, shoeing horses. Pretty much a lazy hombre, Roberto Cherino, even if he is a good farrier. Do you remember him? Berto graduated with us."

She remembered. He'd been the first person to add the "Big" before Tom's "Redd." She made her own attempt at nonchalance by boosting a shoulder. "He's a sawed-off putz, I recall."

"That's Berto."

Feeling the need for closeness, Blythe relaxed to the ground and rolled toward Tom. He looped his arm beneath her shoulders, bringing her closer, saying, "Berto borrowed money from me. Said he'd pay it back when he got his income-tax refund. A few weeks later I heard he was throwing money around town, so I figured to get mine. It was cold that day. You know how it gets in Texas. We always have a cold snap just before Easter. Anyhow, soon as I drove up, I sensed something wrong.

"I knocked. No answer. Heard screams. 'Fire!' I

grabbed a tire iron from the yard—it was that sort of place. Broke the glass pane in the front door. Got it open. Ammanda had lit a propane heater that Roberto had bought, I later found out, with his income-tax refund. The control was defective.''

Blythe shivered, imagining the horror of it all. Hurting for Tom more than anything.

"It was easy," he said, "pulling the first girl free. She was between the door and the blaze. Julia was trapped on the other side of it. Terrified. Huddling in a corner. I dragged her out. We were in pretty good shape.''

"And?" Blythe had trouble breathing. "What happened then?''

"Need I tell you? Hasn't Margaret filled you in?''

"I asked her not to say too much, that I wanted to hear it from you. And I do. Please. What happened after you got the second girl to safety?''

"The girls started crying for their baby cat.''

"Oh, Tom." Blythe pressed her cheek to his chest. She'd gotten the picture, a panoramic snapshot. It went along with Margaret's tale of an exploding heater. Feeling awful, and awfully proud of Tom, she said, "Shelly should be writing a book about you. Everybody's hero. Terrific Tom.''

Blythe had the urge to weep into a hankie, to weep real tears of admiration and adoration. Her hero had put his life in jeopardy to make two little sisters happy.

To save a kitten.

Chapter Ten

"Don't cry," Tom whispered, disliking that he'd brought Blythe to tears. He kissed a droplet from her cheek. "It was just a cat. Matter of fact, it clawed me, when I threw the little dickens to safety. That's a cat for you," he said with a forced chuckle. "It was a Siamese. They're ungrateful creatures."

"I've know legions of men and women who fight for their country, for their beliefs, for any number of reasons, even money. I never knew anyone who put their life on the line for a kitten."

"Ultimate foolishness was what it was, charging into a burning mobile home to save a cat. Seems ridiculous in retrospect. But I did it, and there's no changing that."

"Why did you do it?"

He squinted one eye to look at nothing, then stared at Blythe's shoulder. "The Cherino girls, well, they'd suffered enough. Their mother had taken a powder, and they didn't have much of a dad in Berto. They were crying, soot all over their tiny faces. I heard the kitten meow. I saw its hair singeing. It would have taken a heartless bastard not to try to make those little girls happy.''

"But you've regretted it.''

"There's always another kitty. Well, maybe not. It is, was, whatever, cute. And Julia and Ammanda loved it. I knew I'd saved their lives. I had to save their hearts.''

Tears were spilling down Blythe's cheeks. He brushed them away with his thumb, wishing it was within his power to brush a lot of the past away. "Let's not get silly about something so simple as first instinct.''

"I think you're wonderful.''

He watched her expression, saw such admiration that he thought he might drown in it. "You're good for me, Redd.''

Loving the flush that deepened the tones of her cheeks, he stroked her face. Quite a woman, his Redd. Different, but quite a woman. Maybe it hadn't been so stupid, rushing into that fire.

She lifted his scarred fingers to her mouth, her lips touching the heart of his palm, sending a tremor up Tom's arm. She said, "I've never adored you as much as I do at this moment.''

His damaged hand moved to her throat, stroking. He leaned above her. "You make me feel whole. I love that in you, Blythe.''

"You called me Blythe.''

"Yes. It's a sentimental thing.''

"That was one of your pluses, your ability to feel, to touch and be touched."

"I still need that. I need you, Blythe. Here. Now. Touch me. Let me touch you."

"I think that would be splendid."

He smiled, then took her lips in a kiss that went quickly to heated. She was the joy of his life. He could never let her go, and certainly wouldn't this afternoon. Everything fell away—everything but having her in his arms. And knowing the creek was once more theirs.

He needed to kiss more than her lips. He yearned to caress her flesh and bring her to a fever pitch of desire, longed to be truly whole again. Ached to give more pleasure than he took. Yet reality niggled in. It was daylight. If only they were in a darkened room.

No.

This was where they should make love. At the creek. Their creek. Where they had been virgins, first experiencing the ecstasy of love.

Between kisses, he peeled away her clothes. First her blouse, then her Bermuda shorts. "Not fair," she murmured. "I don't want to be the only one exposed to the light of day. My cellulite, you know."

"I love your cotton candy. You're delicious, Redd."

"So are you."

Yet he worried. He wanted her, ached for her. If she was shocked, though, at seeing the extent of his scars, he... God! He'd never get over it, should he repulse Blythe.

Why couldn't night fall? Or at least clouds darken the sky. There would be no miracles of weather. "I think we ought to wait for this," he uttered, barely able to speak.

"We've waited long enough. This is our moment, ours!"

"What if I make you sick?"

She stroked his face, her fingers lingering on his scars. "It's not your skin that excites me. *You* excite me. You've never repulsed me. But how will you know I'm honest, if you don't give me a chance?"

He steeled himself as she took a more aggressive role, peeling away his shirt, kissing each arm as she went. Cooing and humming as she did so. She took care to kiss his scars.

"You're still beautiful," she whispered.

"To you."

"That's all that matters, isn't it? What I think?"

He smiled. "Yes. You're all that matters."

"We both matter." She tickled his chin. "If you don't quit lying here like a big scared dope, I'm going to cry 'sex therapy!' You know I'm not into that. I'll go back to the house and watch TV."

He laughed, rocking her in his arms, his fears and trepidations vanishing. He didn't adore the body that held Blythe's spirit. He adored... "You know, pussycat. I never told you your best feature."

"Yes, you did. My car."

"I lied. Your best feature is *you*."

She wiggled closer, her presence elevating his pulse, jump-starting his passionate desires. Again, they kissed. And by the time his flesh was totally exposed to light, he knew she'd spoken the truth.

Blythe touched her lips to more of his scars.

And he let her.

Taking over, he stripped her bra and panties. They went back into each other's arms. Between moans of pleasure, they kissed, embraced, did the things that lovers did when they gave and took, then took and gave. They became one again, rejoicing in their reunion of the body, heart and soul.

He didn't remember it being this wonderful.

He had been reborn, a phoenix rising from the ashes.

"You're strutting around like a peacock."

"Go to bed, Granny Myrt."

Blythe shuffled cards, listening to a selection of Myrtle's rock music and that interchange between grandson and grandmother. Tom walked the parlor, looking fantastic. Myrtle, having treated herself to a new perm that afternoon, twirled her finger into a tight curl.

The card table before Blythe, twenty-four hours after she and Tom had made love beside the creek, she dealt a hand of solitaire. But she would prefer to be in his arms. And if Myrtle would *ever* go to bed, that was where she intended to be. It was crazy, of course, getting involved with Tom again.

Life was crazy.

So be it.

She was in love with a guy who'd saved a Siamese.

"Shelly's going with me to California," Myrtle disclosed. "I paid for her ticket this afternoon. Got her an economy ticket. Prudence has an ex-student who works for a travel agent. She was able to pull strings. It pays to know people." Myrtle coyly leaned her chin on a fist. "Did y'all enjoy my boom box?"

Blythe squirmed, figuring every bit of their escapade was written in her face, as it was in Tom's every peacock-like movement. "I recommend it highly," she said.

"Goody. I knew y'all would be in the mood." She got to her feet and did a jig. "What fun, fun, fun in the warm California sun. Warm *Texas* sun."

"It's not like that," Blythe protested.

"Granny, you're embarrassing me."

The dancing stopped. "Don't want to do no embarrassing. I'm going to my room. Need to go through my closet, anyhow, and see what all I need to buy to spiff up my wardrobe. I got one of them lingerie catalogs. Think I'll buy me a red bustier."

"Please," Tom said with a croak, blushing.

"Better yet, think I'll drive over to Prudence's, see if she wants to go to the mall. I'll spend the night at her place, in case y'all want to stay up late, listening to old-fogy music."

Blythe glanced at Tom, catching his slight wink.

Myrtle kept talking. "I wanna buy me one of them strapless dresses, too, just in case Shelly and I get invited to a movie premiere."

Tom chuckled, rolled his eyes. "I don't know how we ever kept her down on the farm, after she'd seen Broadway."

"Ain't those words to a song?"

"Sort of, Granny Myrt. Maybe one even older than you."

"Humph. You're as old as you feel."

Blythe felt younger than young. She knew she loved Tom even more than she had as a kid, but love brought added problems. How could she leave him?

Why was it that she didn't want to?

He had saved a kitten, but what was that in the greater scheme of things? A lot. It symbolized how much Tom was willing to give of himself for a cause.

That was the ultimate aphrodisiac to Blythe.

Would she leave? Tom suspected so. Naked as the day they were born, they made love that night in the dark of his room. They made love again in the gray of morning. Yet he knew. As surely as he knew his name, he knew Blythe would leave, before the weekend rolled around.

Unless he did something to stop her.

Thunder rolled outside their haven, matching the trouble in his veins. Rain pounded the tin roof. This would be a great time to enjoy the…rain.

Forget it. For now.

He decided the only way to reach her was through the sentimental. As they lay in bed with muted light clouding through his bedroom window, he decided to goad her out of leaving. "We never ate our strawberries and apricots."

"They've probably gone bad by now."

"Not the champagne. I've got it on ice."

"It's a bit early for drinking, don't you think?"

"It's five o'clock somewhere in the world." Listening to all that lovely rain, he caressed her thigh. "I could fix us a pot of coffee, though."

"You do the coffee and I'll make some toast."

She started to jump from bed, but he caught her wrist and hauled her back to the mattress. "I want you to know something. The second luckiest moment of my life was when you came back into it."

"What's the first?" She wanted to know.

"The moment I got a gander at your car."

She laughed. "Oh, you. How you do go on. Maybe I adore you for your...hmm? Batting average?"

"We're batting a thousand so far." He stroked her flesh again, murmuring how he loved it. Touching the keloid on her belly, he fell to the dangerous. "I wish this hadn't happened."

"It did, Tom. And it could happen again."

"Not if you don't leave the ranch."

The pelt of rain began, nailing the tin roof like a wild jackhammer.

Ignoring the storm, she said, "I'll have to leave. Any number of things could happen here, even if I stayed. There are no guarantees of safety."

Too bad about the storm. It seemed a shame to waste a summer rain. More than shameful was his determination to change her mind. "Wouldn't it be nice if we both gave up heroics? I'd like to think we could live quietly, enjoying each other and the simple things."

"Like solitaire or dominoes? Like TV dinners and the shopping channel? Like Dairy Divine and the new growth of airplane plant fronds?" She grabbed his robe, put it on, sat on the edge of the bed. "Tom, that's not my scene."

He pulled his jeans on and sat beside her. He might make her happy in bed, but how happy could a yokel make a sophisticated woman? *She's never said a word about loving you.*

He hadn't said it, either. It was too soon for avowals

of love, he told himself. But it wasn't too soon to impress her. He had big ideas; he knew she'd go for them.

First off, he'd make the coffee. Serious talk needed a big shot of caffeine.

The sky outside dark, thunder rolling, rain pouring, Blythe followed Tom to the kitchen and switched on the lights. Coffee was dripping into the pot. Already he'd dropped slices of bread into the toaster. His eyes were full of mischief; his gaze seized her in a divine, dazzling web that knew no reason. She could find something in solitaire and dominoes. She might even learn to cook.

What could she tell Sir Monty?

This has got to stop. You're drunk on passion. Just because he'd saved little girls and a kitty, just because he'd been a good guy for most of his life, didn't quite make up for that empty APO box, or how he'd gone to Dana.

But what would be wrong with making the most of these moments?

Already she was in so deep that there would be no leaving without another hurt. Now wasn't a hurting moment, so she decided to enjoy it. The future, she'd think about later.

Like a waiter puffed with overimportance, Tom slathered marmalade on her toast and filled her cup, then presented them both with flare. "For you, madame."

He sat. Better put, he straddled the back of a chair. His features mobile with some unspoken something, she smiled. How happy it made her, that he could sit before her, shirtless, and be buoyant. He deserved happiness.

After all the wonderful things he'd done in his life, he more than deserved it.

"Should I say, penny for your thoughts?" she asked.

"Nope. I'm cheap. You'll get my thoughts for zip." He took a big bite of toast, washed it down with coffee. After wiping his mouth with a serviette, he said, "I've been thinking about Shelly and Icky. They're like a lot of teenagers. At loose ends. Kids need something constructive to keep them occupied."

"Like what? I can't see kids playing dominoes or getting excited about TV programs."

"They need a meeting place of some sort. A spot to themselves. I've got room. I've got land. I'd like to grade a pasture for a new soccer field."

"Soccer? There is that. But what about baseball? I'd think you'd be interested in baseball."

"Kids are more into soccer nowadays. It's time to move on." He shrugged. "Besides the field, I'm going to remodel the barn into a recreation center."

His generosity overwhelmed her. He would double his standing as China Grove's hero. Yet she knew he was too unpretentious to consider heroism as a reason for his plans. This was Tom, simply being Tom. The old Tom.

With unpretentiousness came naïveté. She sipped coffee, considering the ramifications of his plans. *No good deed goes unpunished.* "You'd take on a huge responsibility. Gifts freely given would spoil children. Further spoil them."

"I've thought about that. Don't you agree it'll be better if we—if I—make them work for their supper?"

"I do. How?"

"The younger ones can foster grade-schoolers or the

old folks at Happy Acres. That's the rest home,'' he explained unnecessarily. ''Teenagers could tutor in reading, or volunteer at the burn center in San Antonio. Or both. There'll be the rec center as reward.''

''Sounds good.''

''I foresee soccer, dances, hayrides. Computers, video gizmos.'' Tom waxed enthusiastic. ''For kids like Shelly, we could organize writing workshops. I hear there're some good authors in San Antonio who like to help kids. There're many ways to go, Redd. I see everything but drugs or rap music. What the hell. I might even give on the rap music, so long as everyone behaves.''

''Not all kids have cars. Or are old enough to drive. You're not exactly in the center of town.''

''If they need transportation, I'll hire a bus or something.''

''I'm proud of you,'' she said sincerely.

''I appreciate your faith in me.''

''You earned it. But let's be practical. What about the financial outlay?''

''What's with the gloom? That's my department.''

''No way on the gloom, Tom. I'm simply trying to help you study the whole picture. You're talking big money.''

''I'm not strapped. Anyhow, I can do most of the fix-up on the barn—I bet I can still wield a hammer and drive a few nails. I've got my settlement from the fire. And the profits from selling acreage. Might as well put it to good work. You did, you know, remind me I owe a debt to the community.''

''There is that.''

''I've even got a name in mind. Phoenix Center.''

"Risen from the ashes. Like you."

"Exactly."

"I like it. I like *you.* You're *très époustouflant.*"

"I was hoping you'd say that." Leaning toward her, he tipped her chin upward with a crook of his finger.

She yearned for more touches, but got practical. "Hold the plane."

He tugged on the robe's sash.

"Are you... Are you doing the center simply to impress me?"

He hesitated. "I'm in the spirit, so why argue over how I got here? It feels good, being my old self. My success is yours. If not for you, I'd still be throwing pecans at people."

"Ah, yes." She did recall a bedraggled hermit with a sorry pitching arm. Such a change. *I've accomplished what I set out to.* Blythe smiled at Tom's positive goal, Phoenix Center.

Then the lights went out.

"Want to make love in the rain?"

"We always did enjoy...rain."

Somewhat later, sated yet insatiable, Blythe rubbed her bare midriff in anticipation of finishing breakfast. "I'm starving. We've worked off calories. I need more marmalade and toast."

He stretched up to kiss one lock of her hair, then another. "Do you know you give a particular gasp..."

"Do I?"

"Every time."

"That's why the French call it the little death, I suppose. I gasp for breath."

"I'll say."

"As much as I enjoy *la petite mort* with you," she said, "I am hungry. We should dress. Your grandmother could drive up and waltz in the kitchen any moment."

"Seems ridiculous at our age, worrying about getting caught with our pants down."

"Doesn't it? It's stopped raining. Let's have a nice omelette, then we'll walk out to the barn and you can show me what you intend to do to make it into Phoenix Center."

He pulled his jeans on and stood, offering a hand to help her to her feet. She shrugged into the robe.

"I was hoping *we* could make it Phoenix Center," he said expectantly.

She might be making the biggest mistake of her life, yet she said, "I'm willing to stay here awhile. Till you get used to Myrtle being gone. Till you start work on the center. But the key phrase is 'awhile.' I can't put off Partners in Crisis forever. I'm needed."

"I need you, too." Tom walked to the kitchen counter. Held on to the edge of it. "Would it make a difference if I tell you..." He whipped around. "I love you."

Hearing his love was like a song chanted by the voices of angels. Hallelujah! How many times over the years had she thought she'd never hear those words again? She could have danced, could have shouted, but wouldn't. He was using his avowal to control her.

"I've known you love me." She'd never acknowledged it, but she'd known, perhaps from that moment he'd stood over her, worried, after lobbing that pecan.

"If you didn't, you wouldn't have let me intrude on your life."

She just didn't know how deep his love went.

If she could trust that he loved her enough...

How could she know?

"I love you so much, Redd, that I can't let you go to Africa. Not to those Partners in Crime people."

"Crisis, Tom. Crisis. It's Partners in Crisis."

"Crisis is the part that worries me."

"You must understand. Nursing is a part of me. It would be like giving up a limb, or a chunk of my heart, to let it go." It had given her life, when she'd been starving herself silly, so hurt that she couldn't even imagine a future.

Exhaling loudly, he rubbed his neck. "You can't grow old hanging from helicopters or devoting yourself to a band of nomadic do-gooders. You and your damn death wish."

"No, Tom. It's a life wish."

"I'm not impressed. But I will say, you could get a job at a hospital. They always need nurses."

"That's taking temperatures and checking pulses."

"Am I not enough excitement for you, Redd? What if I make you a better offer?" He crossed the kitchen, taking her hand, his features intense. "What if I throw in a little flash and dash. I'll buy a Mercedes. I'll learn to eat quiche. I won't make you live in a dump. We'll build a new house. You just pick the kind and size, fill it with whatever you want. I'm not asking you to give up the high life, either. We can travel, or whatever pleases you."

"Ah, yes. Become tourists, sweeping through tourist

traps, breaking local rules of etiquette. Tom, after you've seen a dozen castles, they all start to look the same." The house idea didn't sound bad, though. *Get real.* Four walls could close in, especially in the vicinity of China Grove.

Sheesh. What a pickle. He was the hero who'd saved a kitty. He was the man she had loved most of her life. He was her long, tall Texan. And she was Blythe. Messed up by fifteen years of being ignored. Fifteen years of knowing he'd turned to Dana. Fifteen years of wanting…vengeance? No. At least she hoped not. She couldn't describe what she wanted.

"I need to trust you. Oh, Tom! I don't know what I want, but I know this is an awful mess we're in."

"Granted. Let's unmess it."

"Are you asking me to marry you?"

He blanched. "Marriage? Uh, well. I don't know. I hadn't thought about that."

His reaction hurt, far too deeply than it ought to. "What would it take to make you think about it? Do I have to claim I'm pregnant?" Even as she said those hateful words, she regretted them. "Forget I said that."

"Do you think you might be… Damn. Redd, we haven't been all that cautious. If you are pregnant, I'll be thrilled."

Was that what he'd told Dana? "Children do result from what we've been doing since our afternoon at the creek. But kids are for other people. It's not that I don't think they're divine. They're just not for me."

"What if we've already got one?"

"We don't, Tom. I'm barren."

He blinked. "That explains a lot."

"I'm barren on purpose."

"Fine." He shoved a hand through his hair. "You can't have kids. And I've never hankered for them, not in a long time, anyway. Whatever. I can live with no kids."

"What are you asking of me?"

"That we live together awhile."

"Why?"

He paced the kitchen, up and down, up and down. "You may have had a good marriage, but I didn't."

That he'd had a marriage so soon after Blythe had left—that was the crux of it.

There was a test to his love. "What if... What if you went away with me? To Africa. You could join Partners in Crisis. There's a need for you. You could show other burn victims life after catastrophe. We could be a team. You and me. Me and you. Together, for...however long it lasts. Giving hope, taking satisfaction from our good deeds."

"Do you think I'm crazy?"

"I'd like to think so."

"I don't want to fly off to Africa."

"You saved a kitty. Why wouldn't you want to save mankind?"

"Because I have no desire to save anyone but myself. And you. I can't identify with Africa. We could make a life here, Redd. Just me and you. As time goes by—" he shrugged "—we could talk marriage."

Talk marriage? Anger prickled the back of her neck, seeped into her marrow. He was everyone's hero, except when it came to offering forever to her. Damn him. "I'm leaving. Don't try to stop me."

Tom's features tightened. His gaze went cold as he left the kitchen, throwing over his shoulder, "Then just go."

"Messed up, didn't you?" Myrtle said.

Tom sidestepped his interrogator, making for his bedroom. Home sweet home. Home stale home. Strange, how it seemed so empty when Blythe's heart wasn't in it. She wasn't in at all. She'd gotten into her Porsche and headed out four days ago, her parting words having been a lame apology for breaking their date for next Saturday night's reunion.

He had, nonetheless, watered her plants. He couldn't let them die of neglect, as he was doing. If only she'd stuck around for more do-gooding. Or would turn up to do more of it. No. He couldn't imagine her showing up.

He knew he'd hurt her, not offering marriage. He just wasn't ready for it. But he wasn't prepared to lose her, either, despite his dumb order for her to leave.

He plopped to his bed, his spine to the mattress.

His grandmother, having returned from the learning center, fussed with pillows; she didn't quit with driving him up the wall. "Don't you reckon you ought to get with it on Phoenix Center? It would beat moping around."

"Won't be any Phoenix Center." He had no stomach for it. Not without *her.*

"Blythe made it sound like it'd be real good for you."

"She made a lot of things sound good," he replied, the ache within going even more hollow. Hollow, yet charged with hurt.

His grandmother stroked his brow as if he were a

child. "You just don't see... She did you good. You're a different man than what tried to attack her when she first drove up."

He chuckled mirthlessly. "Yeah, I changed."

He noticed Granny Myrt had done some changing herself. She'd caked her cheeks with red rouge, her mouth made up in what was locally referred to as "whorehouse red." Those were new clothes, too. Platform shoes. *She's ready to rock 'n' roll.*

"You're changed, too," he accused. "She's set you up for a fall."

He expected fireworks. What he got was a look of pity. His grandmother shook her head and dropped to sit at the edge of his bed. "I know I may not succeed in Hollywood. Sometimes it takes years to make it big. I don't have that many years left. Who knows how many years we have left? The thing is, we have to live for today. I just about quit living, when I gave up my little house and garden in town. I'm not looking for sympathy. I wanted to help you. But you can make it on your own now. Like honey girl said, 'It's time for Myrtle.'"

If looks could kill, Myrtle Tillman would be in bad shape.

Give her a break.

He studied his dolled-up grandmother and her curled hair with its purple rinse. Levering from bed, he hugged her. "Good luck in Tinseltown, Granny."

"Thankee, son. Don't you go to worrying. I'm not going to leave you stranded. There's a lady up at my school needs work. She can cook and clean. I hired her to help you."

"I'm not an invalid. Not anymore."

"That's what I've been trying to tell you. Honey girl gave us hope. And strength."

"That she did."

A moment passed before Granny Myrt said, "What're you going to do without her? Think about it. A year from now. Five years. Ten. Do you see yourself alone and lonely?"

Abject panic. Where was Blythe? How could he find her? What would he do once he did?

"Go after her, Tom. Grab her by the arm and haul her in front of a preacher man. You love her. Show it."

How could he find her? "Call Mrs. Packard. See if she knows anyone in the tracking business. Wait. I'll call Ron Dinlum. He tracked her to Florida. I'll bet his people can trace her to Africa."

"That's the spirit."

Tom dashed to the telephone. It took all day to locate the Partners in Crisis team and to make airline reservations to reach them. By noon the next day, Tom had a ticket in his pocket and his bag packed. Just exactly what he'd say once he found her, he had no idea. A proposal of marriage would be a good start.

The moment he took his suitcase to the porch to put it in the pickup for the trip to the San Antonio airport, he saw a fancy red automobile barreling up the road, Blythe Redd piloting the cockpit.

Tom grinned big. "That's more like it."

Chapter Eleven

If the first trek to China Grove had seemed arduous, the lengthier westward return struck Blythe without end. Especially since she'd arrived in London before continuing on to Texas. At last she'd reached Tom.

Nerves jumping, she vaulted from her car. Well groomed and decked out in his cowboy best, with greenery in full foliage around him, he stood on the porch, no pecans in hand.

Yearning to fly into his arms, she climbed the front step, intending to do whatever it took to turn everything into champagne and sunshine. Yet she hesitated, a complete coward. She'd traveled across the Atlantic and back just to panic?

"How's Pickles?" she asked, too nervous to get to the point. "You said she couldn't stay if I wasn't here."

"That old nag is fine. I say a lot." Tom rubbed his jaw. "What happened to Africa?"

Partners in Crisis's cargo plane had shipped light, which meant starving Africans got short shrift from counted-on medical help. She tried to be casual. "I'm sure my team has reached Mbotswaka by now."

"Why aren't you with them?"

"I asked Sir Monty to give me leave to sort through my head. Your head. Our heads."

A slow smile inched across Tom's inscrutable face. "Glad to hear it. Glad you didn't show up ten minutes later, or else we would have…" He reached behind Diablo, sliding a suitcase to his side. "Missed our connection."

What?

"Why, Tom Tillman." Thrilled beyond measure, she rushed into his bear hug. "You were flying after me, weren't you?"

"Marry me, Redd."

He kissed her then, their arms tightening. She said, "That's the most wonderful thing you've ever said."

"Is that a yes or no?"

Say yes, her heart shouted. To accept, though, wouldn't be fair, would force his hand, as it had been forced by Dana. Not under the same circumstances, of course, but Blythe wanted a marriage proposal that hadn't been coerced.

"We should go slowly into marriage, like you suggested," she answered. "If we marry, it should be because we're certain of each other." Certain they could adjust.

"You're right there."

The best part of being right was they were back together. Blythe gave thanks for that, relieved Tom hadn't turned her away. She gave thanks for a period of time to sort through their heads and heart.

They took time to head for the creek.

Later that afternoon Tom led Blythe on a barn tour, explaining his renewed plans for Phoenix Center. His was a strange feeling, ease mixed with trepidation. Did he truly have her? She'd shown up, but where were those three special words?

"I'll start with a new roof," he said, honing in on a noncombative ground. "Won't do the roofing myself. I'll hire a crew of carpenters. I will work along with them. We need a floor, a bandstand, a couple of cozy areas for seminars."

"What about an office?"

"I could turn the stable into one."

"What about Pickles?"

"All right, I give," he said. "I'll have a small office built. I guess I should get an architect in on this."

"Might be a good idea. We wouldn't want the walls caving in on the kids," she teased.

"Will you take charge of the paperwork?" At her nod, he turned pensive. "I wish Shelly weren't leaving. I'd like her in on the plans."

"I stopped in at the Saldivars' on the way from the airport. I'd left my car with Margaret, you see. Whatever the case, I chatted with Shelly for a few minutes. Myrtle was there. I caught them as they were just going out the door for a trip to San Antonio, to buy Shelly some new clothes."

"Did you know Shelly's going to pick up where Readers Center leaves off, tutoring Granny Myrt?" he asked.

"That's what Myrtle told me. Shelly didn't have a lot to say, but she did mention she hasn't heard from Icky."

"I know. I remember what it's like."

He went to the barn door, his back to her; he stared out, the sun casting his long shadow toward Blythe. Yet the pain she'd seen in his eyes lingered within her. He'd been hurt when she'd gone to Germany; it was tough, realizing the depth of it.

"I'm sorry I didn't have the strength to stand up to my father," she said, walking closer to him. "I shouldn't have left you, even if I was underage."

"Or I should have gone after you."

She might not understand Tom's reasons for letting Dana allay his loneliness, might never. It would serve them both if she just lay the past to rest.

By the time the Sweet Creek's idea of dinner hour approached the next evening, Blythe perched and Tom lolled on porch chairs, watching the sun fade to blues and oranges. They listened to the radio on their gift boom box. Just lazing about.

She sipped lemonade, the powdered kind. She could have squeezed lemons for the real stuff, so much energy pinged through her. When the radio announcer switched to the news desk, Blythe's fizz fizzled. The situation in Mbotswaka, according to the news, had worsened.

She punched the Off button. Rather than think about how she'd let down needy people, she said, "What are we going to do about dinner?"

"Dinner? What would you like? We could drive in to San Antonio. I never did take you to a fancy restaurant."

"Another night."

"How about tomorrow night?"

"No. I'm going to cook."

"If I didn't know better," he said, joshing, "I'd ask if you'd been drinking."

"That's a hateful thing to say." She grinned, despite her heavy heart. "I know I'm not known for the domestic scene, but I'm willing to try. I've got to warn you, though. My one and only specialty is asparagus soup."

"Sweet'eart, if you fix it for me, I'll love asparagus soup." He reached to pat her leg. "Provided we have strawberries for dessert."

"I'm game if you are."

"That you'll eat strawberries and I'll eat asparagus, well, that shows we're willing to make big sacrifices for each other."

"Huge sacrifices." With a chuckle, she said, "I'm going to cry uncle. Why torture ourselves? I'll find a recipe somewhere, for something. Myrtle asked me to take her on goodbye rounds tomorrow afternoon. She wants to introduce me to her friends, the ones I don't know. Why don't I ask for recipes?"

"Sounds good."

Not really. Meeting Myrtle's friends ranked with facing a board of inquiry; several of the town folks had been unkind to a lumpy teenager. China Grove had to be gotten used to, though, if—big if!—she and Tom were to end up long-term.

At least she'd have something to say, asking for recipes.

She left her chair to walk behind his chair. Touching his head, she said, "What do you say to making a trip of our own in the morning? Shopping for reunion clothes, and to a barber for you. You really need to do something with this hair. Tom...I hate to say it, but it's time to let go of the ponytail. It looks flat peculiar, poking below cowboy hats. And I prefer you in shorter hair."

"Then I'm barber bound. I'm ready for the new old me." He twisted his head up to look at her. "What are you ready for?"

"The reunion. Better put, for it to be over."

He took her wrist and urged her in front of him, only to pull her onto his hardening lap. "We don't have to attend. We could make our own party."

"No." Blythe shook her head. "We both need to face the old crowd. In truth, Tom, I need to be there. If nothing else, to prove to myself that sticks and stones don't hurt me."

For supper the next night they ate a delicious pot of beef stew, prepared by Blythe. Well, Tom proclaimed it delicious. It was way undercooked. The beef could have served as boot leather. Carrots and potatoes, hard as stones, swam in enough tomatoey grease to send a cast-iron stomach to a Maalox moment. Granny Myrt ate a half bowl, then cried Maalox. Tom ate three.

In hindsight he'd have preferred Blythe to make her dinner specialty: reservations.

"You did great," he complimented again as he patted

his stomach for the umpteenth time while they did the dishes.

"Mmm, thanks."

She'd been uncharacteristically quiet all day and into the evening. Matter of fact, she'd been that way since hearing about Africa. It might be of her own accord, her presence, but Tom knew she pined for her partners. She loved her work. Yet she hadn't as much as whispered "I love you" to him.

And she still wore her wedding band.

Don't make too much of it. But it was difficult not to do.

This morning he'd almost gotten her in a good mood. First, he'd visited a barber. Afterward, they went to San Antonio's best Western store to select his reunion duds. Next had been a pricey ladies' shop. He'd enjoyed helping her pick out a flattering sundress and bolero jacket of deep green, with high-heel sandals to match. They had lunched at the best restaurant on the River Walk. In her element she'd been ebullient.

The ranch was not her element.

"Anybody for a round of moon?" his grandmother called into the kitchen.

"You up to a dominoes game?" he asked as his sweetheart wiped her hands on a tea towel, then needlessly brushed her shorts and top with the heel of her hand.

"Sure. Why not?"

"Set up the card table, Granny."

Wanting to keep the conversation light, he shuffled facedown dominoes, saying, "You two must've visited half Granny Myrt's friends, asking for recipes."

"Them old battle-axes," his grandmother grumbled. "Nestor's wife give Blythe a once-over and said, 'I don't know any low-fat recipes.' Humph. As if we'd asked. I'm off on Prudence, I'm telling ya. That crone had the nerve to hint that our honey girl ought to get one of them diet cookbooks."

Tom groaned, slicked his hand along newly cropped hair. It was hard enough, making Blythe happy, without having people yap about her weight. Although sticks and stones didn't much faze her healthy attitude about her weight, he'd have a healthier attitude, if people would accept her, as she accepted herself.

Blythe scanned her dominoes, lining up the dotted sides to face her. She said to his granny, "We did get many good recipes from the other ladies, and you've promised to write yours down. You're doing so well with reading and writing. I'm very proud of you, Myrtle." She looked up to smile. "You'll be reading romance novels and I'll be a cook in no time."

Granny Myrt lifted game pieces to arrange them in one palm. "I ain't one for lying. I'm glad I'm going to California. I don't want to be in any more cooking experiments. I love you, honey girl, like you're my own, which you are in a way, but I have to tell ya, I'm leaving my stomach to trained hands. Gonna take myself and Shelly to Spago the minute we hit Tinseltown."

Blythe tossed a double-six to the table, winning the round. "Can't blame you, Myrtle. That is a great restaurant. If you don't mind rubbing elbows with celebrities."

"Can't say that I would. I'm hoping to see Paul Newman. That boy always did it for me. I wouldn't mind if he ate crackers in my bed."

"He is very nice. So is his wife."

"You know those kinds of people?" Tom asked, incredulous.

"Some. Tom, are you going to play or not?"

He played, but... Damn!

Blythe won the hand with a double-five.

Old fingers scratched into blued hair. One look at the rest of her dominoes and Granny Myrt grumbled. "I dunno how one woman can get such lousy bones. I'll be glad to get to La La Land. Ain't never gonna pick up another domino. This is a real country game. No more poop-kickin' for this chick."

Planning to roll his eyes again, Tom cut a glance at Blythe. His brow tightened. Before she schooled it, he'd seen a look of overt boredom in her eyes.

Such a fool he'd been, thinking she'd adapt to the ho-hum of South Texas. She needed bright lights and fawning waiters, gunfire and the heroics of battlefield rescues. How in the hell could he give her what she needed?

Before this visit Blythe hadn't been one to worry about trips to the beauty shop.

"Blythe Redd? I'm going to do Blythe Redd? As I live and breathe."

Of all the luck. Bad luck. Blythe groaned. Her first visit to Kurleen's Kut and Kurl on her arrival in town, women had lined up to await Kurleen's scissors. This afternoon she was the sole client, Kurleen nowhere in sight. If *this* hair stylist did her anything like she'd done in high school, Blythe would have been better off patronizing the Woof Clipper.

The hairdresser was none other than Edna Cook, former majorette and bosom buddy to Dana McCabe.

"Where's Kurleen?" Blythe asked the beauteous blonde for whom fifteen years had been kind.

"Sick. Stomach flu. I'm taking her appointments."

"With the reunion tonight, I figured this place would be packed."

"Everyone got their hair done earlier, if at all. You're my last customer of the day." Pretty features looked insulted. "I'd heard you were back, and wanted to get my hands on you."

Exactly. Blythe backed toward the door. "I didn't see you here last time."

"I was on vacation." Long orange nails sporting silver stars on each, with an arm of bangle bracelets, motioned toward the shop's rear. "I can do you much better than Kurleen did."

That's what I'm afraid of. Run!

"Ms. Cook, I'm down for a cut," Blythe said, deciding on the formal, wary of those hate-filled fingers wielding scissors. "I'm canceling. Don't have time. Busy schedule. Sorry."

"Poteet. I'm Edna Poteet now. Married Charlie Poteet, right out of beauty school. And don't you dare cancel. Kurleen would have my head on a platter. How about I just give you a wash and blow-dry? That won't take any time." Edna pointed past rows of beauty products and pictures of models in a myriad of hairstyles. "Follow me to that shampoo chair at the rear."

Starred fingers clamped Blythe's wrist formidably. It wasn't every day that anyone could strong-arm Blythe Redd anywhere, but Edna Poteet did.

She propelled her to the chair before the shampoo sink. "I'll fix you up, pretty as a picture. You're going to the reunion, I know you are. Margaret told me. We'll have you looking so good, not even Tom will recognize you."

"That's what I'm scared of. You stood beside the leaders of the pack, making fun of me in school." Blythe protected her hair with covering hands. "You'll make me a laughingstock!"

"Head back." Marine corps generals would envy Edna's commanding voice. She softened it. "I'm not going to scalp you. Or scald you. I promise not to cut so much as a split end."

"Fine. Not so much as a split end."

Blythe's head wet, Edna soaped it, using strong fingers. "Do you hold it against me, Dana being my pal?"

"Why should I trust you?"

Edna trained the water nozzle, then added a second application of shampoo. Rinsing for the final time, she said, "You may not believe this, but I didn't like the way Dana made fun of you. Dana doesn't understand imperfection. Her idea of imperfection, that is. It wasn't so much that she found you lacking, she was jealous. I realized that, once she bagged Tom. I'm glad she took off and didn't come back."

At least the beauty was honest.

She led Blythe to her station, seating her before a mirror that had numerous photographs of kids taped to it. Blythe was too worried about her hair to study those cute faces.

"Listen, Big Redd—"

"Please don't call me Big Redd. I don't like it."

"It is juvenile. Sorry, Blythe." Edna turned her gaze this way and that, assessing red hair. "I can't stand it." Scissors magically appeared. "I've just got to trim right here."

Distrusting, Blythe's hands again jerked up to protect her head. "Don't you dare!"

"Put your hands down, Blythe. This minute."

"The marines could use a few good women like you."

"Isn't that the truth?" She laughed. "I should have joined, rather than going to beauty school."

The chair swiveled to face the window. Hair flew. As Edna wielded steel, Blythe cringed, fearing she'd for sure end up a laughingstock at the reunion, if her hair fears came to fruition.

The hair-dryer hot against her scalp—probably her naked scalp!—Blythe bemoaned, "What have you done to me?"

Those starred fingertips worked this way and that to fluff and arrange. A can of hair spray misting her creation, Edna spun the chair. "Like it?"

Blythe's eyes widened in the mirror. "Yikes!"

Her chin on line with Blythe's shoulder, Edna studied the mirror's reflection. "Gorgeous, isn't it?"

"Thank you, Edna," Blythe said with a satisfied smile. "My hair's never looked spiffier."

"Knock 'em dead at the reunion, girl."

Why not be upbeat? Tonight Blythe would show China Grove a thing or two. Mainly, how Tom Tillman had risen from the ashes. All right, she'd also be showing this town that she'd done just fine, thank you very much. Yeah, right. "Why should I even care what they think?" she mumbled.

After dressing for the reunion, she entered the parlor, where Tom waited. Looking dashing as the dickens, he whistled. He tossed his Stetson to a table and crossed the floor to place his hand at the small of her back and pull her to him.

"What's wrong?" he asked.

"I thought I was prepared for ribbing and snubbing. I'm a little scared. Don't get me wrong, Edna Poteet wasn't ugly to me, but...what if they laugh at us?"

"No one's going to laugh. Stare and point, maybe. But they won't laugh." He kissed her cheek. "It's not too late for us to cancel. We're all dolled up. We could do dinner in San Antonio. I hear the food is great at the Fig Tree. It overlooks the River Walk. I hear they serve real caviar and keep a couple busy for hours, eating and being pampered. Of course, if we did, we'd miss barbecue and frozen margaritas served in an old automobile agency. And you'd miss your opportunity to see how many of our old classmates have changed."

"What a switch, your trying to get *me* to the reunion."

"I've got faith in you, pussycat. You'll do fine. Truth to tell, this reunion will do us both good."

"Put that way, how could I resist?"

Her usual erotic scent wafting, her makeup artfully accenting her green eyes, Blythe wore her new duds. Tom proudly escorted her into the former Chevrolet house, where a DJ provided music and the scent of barbecue drifted. As soon as they entered the door, he caught sight of crepe paper streamers and banners. And classmates who were decked out in everything from Western duds and halter tops to suits and dresses.

Despite his pep talk to Blythe, he had the sudden urge to back off. He didn't want to hear anything from anyone, pro or con, about the fire.

He glanced at Blythe. She looked okay, was smiling, didn't seem nervous. He knew she was. She studied the faces, seeking reactions.

"They look pretty good." Her gaze went to a man with a crepe paper streamer draping the shoulder of his Hawaiian shirt. "Well, Ted Acheson looks like warmed-over death."

"True. Sweet'eart, remember—I've got faith in you."

She smiled. "Thank you, Tom."

Margaret Saldivar, leaving her husband at the margarita machine, wove through a crowd that was closing in on Tom and Blythe. "There you are, there you are." She flailed skinny arms, loping like Olive Oyl to them, grinning toothily.

Everyone else gawked, as if they didn't know what to say. The crowd kept a short distance. Tom said, "Howdy, everyone."

Blythe gave a small five-fingered wave.

Margaret clamped her arm. "The photographer's taking pictures of friends. I want one of me and you, before I do something stupid like spill barbecue sauce on my new white dress. Let's get in line."

"Go," Tom said.

They went. The crowd turned, watching as the two women disappeared down the corridor to the former service department, where the photographer had apparently set up shop.

At loose ends, Tom listened to the eclectic mix of music for a few minutes, then ambled to the bar that used to be the parts department counter. He ordered a Big Red. Too caught up in reuniting, people weren't sitting at the folding tables. He took a seat by himself.

Acheson strolled up, margarita in hand. From the dissipation in his jowls and that streamer hanging from his shirt, he appeared on a first-name basis with several margaritas. "Big Redd sure has changed," he said. He slouched into a chair and lit a cigarette, showing well-manicured but shaky hands. "I understand she's made a name for herself."

"I understand you ran into her a while back. Made a comment about her weight. Keep your mouth shut about it."

"I was just trying to drum up some business for my wife." He took a big drag on the cigarette. "My little woman sells diet stuff."

"Make sure she doesn't try to sell it tonight."

Tom decided it was high time to find Blythe. Making his way into the car house's belly, he got stopped by a couple of men. They looked familiar but he couldn't place them.

"Big Redd turned out great," one commented.

"There's a spark in her that wasn't there before. Self-confidence, I guess. Why wouldn't she have it? She's been living large in Europe."

"It's star quality," the other guy said.

Tom smiled at those comments.

He approached the line. Blythe and Margaret were

being posed for their picture. He heard more comments. And was relieved to be basically ignored.

"Isn't she amazing, Heather? I envy Blythe. Her life is like a storybook."

"I'd heard the ugly duckling turned into a swan. Wow."

"Wish I lived glamorous, like she does."

"She's had all sorts of adventures. Margaret told me. Most fun thing I've ever done? Camping at Enchanted Rock."

"I wish I had the nerve to speak to her, to apologize for being nasty to her in school. I'm afraid she'll snub me."

"Me, too," more than one person said.

"She's a celebrity, you know," Arlene Dinlum, a vivacious brunette, said to Edna Poteet, their backs to Tom. "After Ron and I found out she works for Partners in Crisis, we did some asking. European newspapers run stories on her all the time."

"I know all about it, Arlene. You told Margaret, and Margaret told me."

"I don't know what in the world she sees in Tom Tillman. I mean, he used to be fantastic, but what has he done lately?"

"How quickly you forget," Edna said. "Tom charged into a fire. And he coached your kid in softball. Mine, too. He taught Sunday school, and loaned money to anyone who needed it. People who make the news in European papers don't necessarily help those of us in China Grove. Besides, it's something, his turning up at the reunion. That takes courage."

Tom stepped back, not wanting to hear more.

Finished posing for the photographer, Blythe walked toward the gossipers. Since she hadn't heard the accolades, didn't know her old taunters were in awe, Tom knew it took guts for her to smile and lie, "It's nice to see you all again."

She extended her hand toward someone. It wasn't taken in a handshake. Mike Zenkowski grabbed her in a bear hug, booming, "Ain't you a purty lookin' thang? Welcome home!"

"Food's ready," Ron Dinlum boomed from the DJ's microphone. "Come and get it! Last man there does the dishes."

A mad exodus to the caterer's steam tables quickly followed.

Tom couldn't get near Blythe. A flock of men and women surrounded her, offering to fill her plate. He did manage to wedge a chair in at her table. She ate heartily. Tom wanted her smiling and laughing. The more she did, the happier she'd be.

As soon as she finished off a helping of banana pudding, one of her male followers asked her to dance.

Contemplating the steel machine that revolved with margarita mix, Tom decided to have one. He ignored Roberto Cherino's approach. Berto bellowed, "Tomas! You hogging the margaritas?"

Tom moved aside, so the thirsty farrier could fill a plastic glass with the tequila, Cointreau and lime concoction before turning on short bowed legs to eye the dancers.

"Mmm-mmm. That Big Redd, she's got the nice knees," Berto said.

Tom followed her admirer's gaze. Hair swept up as

much as short hair could be, she did the macarena with Jerry Sheperd, the hem of that deep-green dress kicking past her knees.

"Yeah, nice knees." She did have nice knees. "But I wouldn't call her Big Redd, not if I were you. She didn't like it in school and she likes it less now."

"Why not?"

Tom told him. Berto slapped the heel of his hand against his forehead. "That's not what I meant at all." He muttered something in Spanish. "I gotta apologize."

"Do that." Tom pulled the brim of his hat down a mite.

But Berto had something else to say. "Tomas... I came over to talk to you for a reason. I've been wanting, well, I never did get the chance to thank you for saving my daughters."

That.

Damn.

Change the way you think.

Tom took Berto's measure. He felt like letting loose with charges of bad fathering and reckless behavior. If Berto had been on the scene, he wouldn't have gone into that trailer house. Wouldn't have gotten toasted over a stupid cat.

He again ordered himself to change his thinking.

"No big deal," he said.

"You may look at it that way, but I don't. You not only saved my *hijas,* you saved me. I cleaned up my act, moved to North Texas. Took parenting classes. Found a steady job. Got Ammanda and Julia in day care. They're in school now, but they go to the center after class. Thank you for opening my eyes."

For a long time Tom had equated the fire with saving that kitten and his cowardly actions and reactions in the aftermath of it. Suddenly he took pride in his deed. "How's the cat?"

"Got kittens. Want one?"

"No!"

Berto moved on.

"Stardust" played. A cry went up, demanding country-and-western music. The DJ promised the next tune would be by Garth Brooks. Feeling good, Tom decided to cut in on the dancers.

Once his arms were filled with Blythe, he said, "This is our song. Having a good time?"

"Oh, yes." She grinned. "Can you imagine? I think people are in awe of me. They're so easily impressed."

"They are not."

"What about you?" Her grin faded. "Are you okay?"

"Doing fine." He rubbed his hand along her spine, loving the feel of it. "Really fine."

"Don't you think tonight would be a good time to announce your plans for Phoenix Center?" she asked, one of the colored lights at the ceiling hitting the diamonds on her left hand, sparkles that he tried to ignore.

"If you don't make an announcement," Blythe warned, "Margaret may beat you to it. She got it out of Granny Myrt. You don't want Margaret to steal your thunder, do you?"

"I don't know why Southwestern Bell bothered to install telephones in China Grove. Something needs said, she gets the message out. So what? She got you here in the first place. I should thank her."

Blythe snuggled closer. "You really are something."

He nuzzled her ear. "You smell good."

"My usual fragrance. Essence Douze. Fragrance twelve."

He still stroked her spine. "Plain name."

"Ah, but you don't understand. It's been blended in Grasse, France, to a secret formula for the past two centuries. No one outside the family is allowed to use it."

Tom figured the Redds didn't have any such august family recipes floating around. She meant the Ricards. Before she'd shown up to reclaim him from the living dead, she'd had quite a life, one that had made the papers. She might not be a wafer-thin model on the covers of magazines, but she'd made quite a splash in international circles.

"I bet fragrance twelve doesn't smell half as good on anyone else in the 'family,'" he said, feeling alone and lonely, on the periphery of her dazzle.

The song ended. Tom exhaled with relief when one of the men asked for the next number, a swing dance. She and Mike Zenkowski took to the floor.

Tom was more than ready for another margarita. He beat a retreat to fill a glass from the machine. Downed it in one gulp, which froze his soft palate. Just deserts for trying to drown his uncertainties in tequila.

Flora Zenkowski, former cheerleader now stuffed into a dress a size too small, wiggled up to him. "You're sure lookin' good, Tom. Those scars of yours don't look too bad. Do they hurt?"

"Only when someone comments on them."

"You know, sugar—" she patted his jaw "—you better watch out or that scowl's going to lock your face."

"You don't look too happy yourself."

Flora stared at her husband as he danced with Blythe. His smile as wide as Texas, Mike hung on his partner's every word. "My hubby's too gone on your girl. She's a glamour-puss. How can I compete? I've got five kids, corns and stretch marks."

"You look great," Tom exaggerated.

"I groom dogs at the Woof Clipper. I come home smelling like flea shampoo. I bet Blythe always smells like flowers. No way can I compete with a redhead that lives like a heroine in a book. Margaret says Shelly's writing a book about her."

Speaking wryly, Tom said, "Bet you never figured this night would come, when you'd eat your hateful words from high school."

Flora used the small plastic straw to stir her drink. "I hear Big Redd's going to win one of the awards tonight."

Tom smiled, big with pride for his favorite redhead. "This is truly her night."

Yes, it was Blythe's night, a dazzling spectacle of stardom in a defunct auto agency in a podunk Texas town. Tom didn't begrudge her yet another fifteen minutes of fame. He was proud for her glory. Yet...

Before she'd turned up at Sweet Creek, she'd lived her life as if it were a movie. Humble beginnings, the expected struggle, the ultimate acclaim. Time to wake up, Tillman. *Show her you love her enough to give her back to the life she deserves.*

Give her back? Hell, she'd only loaned her time. It was as obvious as that circle of diamonds on her fingers.

China Grove was not for Ms. Redd.

Chapter Twelve

What a night! Blythe squinted into the ladies' room mirror, twisted a lipstick tube up, ran the tip across her lips and eyed the only other person in the rest room. "I still can't believe everyone has been friendly."

Margaret checked her teeth in the mirror, sucking them. "I suspected it would be this way."

Slipping the lipstick case together, Blythe said with a smile, "I expected the same old treatment. I never expected for people to act as if they're interested in me."

The loo's swinging door opened; Edna Poteet waltzed in, a vision in starred fingernails and peacock-blue eye shadow. "Goody! I found you," she said. "Oh, hi, Margaret. Listen, Blythe, you left the shop this afternoon before I could ask a favor." She hoisted a pen and a cocktail napkin. "Could I have your autograph?"

"What?"

As Blythe stood bemused, Margaret, obviously sensing something dishy, roosted on the wide washbasin's counter.

"The autograph's for my daughter, Molly." Edna set the supplies next to Margaret to reach for the evening bag that was tucked under her arm. She dug inside, found a photograph and extended it. "That's Molly. She's fourteen."

Margaret craned her neck to take a look. "That's Molly, all right. Before she went on that diet that made her sick. The no-vitamins, low-protein one that a lot of the girls were trying last semester. Edna, I told you she'd make herself sick."

"Margaret, would you mind terribly if I have a private moment with Blythe?" Edna asked politely, but it was plain she didn't appreciate the criticism.

"I'm leaving. I'll be at our table, Blythe," Margaret said. Earlier, Tom and Ed had staked a table for four for the two couples.

Blythe eyed the photo. The teenager was one of the duo who'd stared at her at Dairy Divine that evening she'd gotten the chocolate ice cream fix. She was quite a bit heavier in this picture.

"Molly has a hard time keeping her weight down," Edna explained. "She lives on Ensuromedic Lite, now that she knows she can get sick from fad diets. I've tried to tell her weight is a state of mind, that attitude makes a difference. She wouldn't listen. Not till you came home. You're such an inspiration. She saw you at Dairy Divine and was absolutely gaga, but she didn't have the nerve to introduce herself."

"I thought she was making fun of me."

"Never."

Quite a revelation. It wasn't smart to make judgment calls, she realized. She'd been guilty of that, same as those who couldn't see past her fat. "Wonders never cease."

"I'd like for you to meet Molly. It would be so nice if you two could get acquainted." As Edna spoke, she took the liberty of picking at Blythe's hair with the tips of those long fingernails, making sure her creation was at its best. "You'd be a good influence. A celebrity with her head on straight."

Blythe chuckled. "Nurses aren't celebrities."

"You're like no nurse China Grove has ever seen."

"Nurses don't give autographs."

"You're a celebrity in the Poteet household. And you are to our classmates. Don't be surprised if it's not formally recognized before this night is over. You're our star."

"I can't believe my ears." Star treatment for the least popular girl in school. "I'm...I'm flabbergasted."

Edna lifted pen and paper. "How about that autograph?"

Feeling idiotic with glee, Blythe signed. She veritably floated from the loo. Who would have ever believed...

Who would have imagined Roberto Cherino would step in front of her, before she could reach the table where Tom sat?

"Want to dance?" he asked.

She'd rather two-step with a billy goat, but this was a night to enjoy, so she let him lead her onto the floor.

"You sure are lookin' good, Blythe."

"You always called me Big Redd. You started the fad."

He flushed. "Never meant it as an insult. Tom called you Redd. My favorite drink is Big Red. You were sweet as soda pop."

"You're kidding."

"No. I'm not."

They continued to dance, and it wasn't half bad. Actually, Berto bolstered her ego even higher. Once he'd escorted her back to Tom, where he sat alone, the Saldivars still on the dance floor, Berto lifted her knuckles and kissed her fingers gallantly. "You made my night," he proclaimed.

"Thanks, Berto."

"What was that about?" Tom asked, his expression strange.

"I think I'm dreaming."

Ron Dinlum, his nice face and kind eyes never appearing more friendly, took that moment to stroll up. "Having fun?"

"You did a fantastic job of organizing this reunion," Blythe said. "Thanks for going to the trouble to track me down."

He bowed. "It's not often we have a star in our midst."

Fawning had begun to get old. Not!

Ron took off, going to the DJ's headquarters where he began to announce the nonsense awards that she supposed all reunions had.

"What was it you were saying about 'dreaming'?" Tom asked, after the Most Children Award went to the girl who'd been pegged in high school as Girl Most Likely To Succeed.

Tom had won the complementary award as a senior.

He tipped up a Big Red can. "Talk to me."

"I can't believe this night. I never, ever dreamed..." She smiled. "Berto had a lot to say when we were dancing. He jeered in school as a defense tactic." She recalled their sophomore year, when she'd tutored the Hispanic boy in Algebra, after their teacher coerced her into it. "Berto said he wanted to ask me out, but figured I'd never date a 'pip-squeak,' so he made fun. It was all in self-defense."

"Sounds reasonable."

"I didn't believe him, not at first. But he said, 'Why would I lie?' His eyes were earnest. He even said it took him until now to get up the nerve to ask for a dance."

"What a guy, to borrow another of your phrases."

Blythe ignored the barbed edge of Tom's tone. "I never told you, but...I once got an unsigned love letter. There was a bluebonnet in the envelope. I didn't meet my 'secret admirer' at Dairy Divine, like the note suggested. I thought it was a sick joke. That's why I never mentioned it. But it wasn't a joke. Berto sent the letter and flower."

"You were always a winner," Tom said tenderly. "You just never realized it."

Before she could ask if something was wrong, Ron Dinlum spoke into the DJ's microphone, getting electronic feedback. "Could I have your attention again, please?"

Squeeeeeeak.

Tom took a sip of red soda. "Not exactly the Georges Cinq in Paris, is it?"

"And the winner for Most Changed goes to..." At the makeshift podium, Ron Dinlum reached for a trophy. "Blythe Redd!"

A cheer went up.

Tom started to slide his scarred hand over her knuckles, but moved it to his lap. "Congratulations, sweet'eart. Go up there and get your award."

She was shocked. Absolutely dumbfounded. Maybe it was true. Her old classmates did admire her. "I hope I don't make a fool of myself, accepting."

"Just say thank you."

"Go with me. Tell everyone about Phoenix Center. Come on, Tom. Let's make this *our* success. You deserve it, too."

"No, sweet'eart. This is your night."

Was this her night?

Upon returning to the ranch, Blythe insisted on a midnight stroll along the creek. She kicked off her shoes and got rid of her panty hose to walk barefoot. Tom followed her to the creek, but continued to act peculiar. Detached. As if something bothered him.

"Someone was ugly to you," she surmised aloud.

"Would you please let up? No one hurt my feelings."

"Then why are you acting weird?" She sat on the bank.

He bent to sit beside her. The scent of his aftershave had waned over the evening, but he still smelled good to her. She inched closer to him, and asked, "What's wrong?"

"Nothing."

She doubted that, but wouldn't argue. The evening being a strong aphrodisiac to her, especially in Tom's presence, she twisted toward him. Her palms planted on either side of him, she brushed her cheek against his jaw. "If you'd make love to me, I'd be the happiest woman on planet earth."

"Would you?"

"Yes."

"Dear, crazy Redd." He guided her back to the grass and levered above her. Cuddled her. "If there's anything I can do to make you happy, I'll do it. Including this."

His lips met hers. Furtively, he nudged his tongue past her teeth, taking a deep and passionate kiss. Soon, they were all arms, each moaning for more.

He peeled off their clothes between kisses. They rolled in the grass, the smell sweet, the scent turning to the erotic perfume of desire. "I want to kiss you everywhere," he murmured, after he had cherished first one breast then the other. "I want you so bad I hurt."

"No hurting," she whispered. "Not tonight. Do anything but hurt."

He worked at it.

The next morning, the day Myrtle and Shelly were leaving on their great adventure, Blythe sensed something was definitely wrong. Last night, after they had made love by the creek, Tom had again turned quiet, too quiet, but she'd chalked it up to fatigue. Today she knew differently.

Waiting for the Los Angeles-bound flight to be called

in the newest of San Antonio's two airport terminals, Blythe prayed that whatever troubled Tom would cease.

They were a quiet foursome, the unhappy happy couple and the westbound travelers. If Ed and Margaret had come along for the send-off, surely someone could have kept chatter going. Unfortunately, Nipster had been experiencing a bad day, so the Saldivars said their adieus at home.

With nothing else to do, Blythe observed the setting. Above the drone of passengers in this wing of the airport, a female's voice over the P.A. system asked for a wheelchair to meet a flight. Three little boys played hide-and-seek beneath the rows of gray seats that lined Gate 6, disturbing various people in turn but staying away from Blythe and her silent companions.

"Anyone for a cup of coffee?" she asked to make conversation, while Shelly flipped through a teen magazine and Tom, his expression hidden by Stetson's best, watched a rerun of "The Beverly Hillbillies" on Southwest Airlines's TV monitor.

Myrtle stood and dusted her fanny. "Let's go to the bar. My nerves is up. Never rode in a plane afore. Don't give a hoot if Southwest is the safest airline on earth, I'm scart."

Tom's gaze left Jethro and Miss Hathaway; he crossed arms over his chest. "Shelly's a minor. I'm not taking a minor to a bar. It's bad training."

"Why does everybody try to run my life?" Shelly bemoaned.

"Hush, girlie-cue. We'll have a good time, once we hit L.A." Myrtle flounced by, her armadillo-shaped purse swinging at her side. "I'm going to the bar by myself. Y'all watch my suitcases. I don't want no sticky-fingered so-and-so grabbing my new clothes. 'Specially my new red bustier.''

"I'll go for the coffees," Blythe offered.

"I'll get them." Tom got to his feet and sauntered off.

Once he'd disappeared down the corridor to a refreshment kiosk and Shelly had a moment alone with Blythe, the girl said, "I wish Icky would show up. I want to go to Hollywood, but I'd rather be with Icky."

"I know." Blythe reached to hug the girl, sharing her dark mood. "Love isn't easy."

"You ought to know. Tom's not making it easy for you. He's been a creep, ever since you showed up."

"That's not true, Shelly. He's wonderful."

"Maybe in your book, but not in mine." Her mouth went petulant. "Besides, you're screwing up the end of my book. Finales need excitement."

If a love story could end on a down note, boy! would Shelly have a story. *Don't be a pessimist.*

Suddenly a smile worked its way onto Shelly's face. Fingers lifted to her cheeks, she said breathily, "Blythe, there's Icky."

A goateed young man, wearing a neatly pressed shirt and nicely fitting trousers, made his way toward them, his gait slow, his arm in a sling. Icky Kuleska, somehow, had known to be at the airport at the reckoning hour.

"Icky!"

"Shelly." He spread his sling, opened his other arm; his girl bounced to his chest.

"I'm gonna miss you," he said, and squeezed her arm.

Icky had turned up, just to let Shelly leave? Just like that?

Tom returned with the coffees, the cups ignored. He sat back down and stared.

"Shelly, hope you don't mind if I never make it big in rap music. I did some thinking, realized I needed to clean up my act. I've got a job in San Antonio, a real job with educational benefits. My boss is gonna send me to electronics school. I've got a place to live, too. You go on, baby. Do your Hollywood thing. Then come back to me. Just promise you won't take up with some Hollywood stud."

"I promise."

Myrtle, looking less frazzled, strolled up and belched behind her hand. "Them margaritas pack a punch. What're you doing here?" she asked Icky.

"Giving my babe a send-off."

"Just don't get no funny ideas. She and I're gonna do Hollywood." A moment passed before Myrtle lifted a brow at Shelly. "Ain't we?"

"I'll do Hollywood," the girl answered. "Then I'll be back to be Icky's... To be whatever he wants."

She kissed the boy then, and they were doing so much hugging and smooching that Blythe worried he'd hurt his bandaged arm.

The gate attendant announced the flight.

Icky and Shelly engaged in another lingering kiss. "I love you, babe," he said, and blew her another kiss when she joined Myrtle to walk down the jetway.

Then he cut away, disappearing down the corridor that led to the main terminal.

Blythe at his side, Tom started up the same corridor, and said, "Shelly didn't have to get on that plane."

"No one *must* do anything. The only givens in this world are death and taxes."

"And wars."

Reaching the boutiques that lined the main terminal, Blythe moved her clutch purse to the other hand, not surprised that his profile was a case study in sourpuss. "Why do you mention that?"

"Reckon it'll take Shelly fifteen years to return?"

Oh, boy. Tom was dredging up the past. Again her handbag got shifted. "She'll be back for school."

"That's what she says."

"I get it. You equate Shelly and Icky with us, but things aren't the same." They reached the down escalator. "Anyhow, all's well that ends well."

"What if she meets some other guy and stays in Hollywood?"

"You're grabbing at straws."

"If she does come back, it could be by red sports car. Or limousine," he added as if he'd tasted something sour.

"I know you didn't like my renting a limo for our trip to the airport. I didn't want to borrow the Saldivars' only vehicle—what if they needed to take the Nipster to the vet? Anyway, we couldn't squeeze into my car or your pickup. And why huddle in a taxi?"

"Just exactly how rich are you?"

"I'm not rich." Except in enthusiasm. "I'm comfortable is all. If I want to hire a limo, I can."

"Forget the limo." The electric door glided open; Tom stomped to the curb. "I'm talking about choices."

Their chauffeur pushed his hip from the front grill of the stretch limousine he'd parked under the No Parking sign. He did the door thing for Blythe and Tom; they climbed in. Once the big conveyance steered from the terminal, she punched the button to close the privacy window.

"What do you mean, choices?" she asked Tom.

Tom shifted on the plush leather seat. Elbow on an armrest, he shelved his upper lip with a forefinger and trained his line of sight out the window. "I'm making a choice."

"And it's..."

"I want you to go back to Partners in Crime."

"Crisis."

He pressed the privacy window button. "Pull over, man. I'm getting out. Leave me at the Diamond Shamrock station on Broadway."

"Are you nuts?" Blythe folded her arms across her chest.

"I think so."

The limo eased off Loop 410 and cruised beneath the gasoline station's canopy. Tom shot to the pavement. He was nuts.

"Drive," Blythe ordered the limousine man. They hadn't gotten back on the service road before she said, "Stop."

She did her own exiting. In his haste to escape, Tom collided with a hulk stepping from the store. Green discount coupons flew from one of the bruiser's mitts, a paper cup of soft drink splashing on his gray-and-green uniform and across the name tag etched Carl. He yelled at Tom. But the scarred cowboy kept going.

Marching down Broadway Street, Blythe approached his trim backside. Cars whizzed by, a truck kicking up enough back draft to upset Tom's hat and the skirt of Blythe's dress. He didn't retrieve the Stetson.

Her hand clamped his shoulder. "Not another step, buddy boy."

He shrugged off her fingers, kept going.

"Be that way. But I'm not taking another step until you're ready to talk." Unfortunately she'd issued an ultimatum in a less than propitious locale. She'd have to sit on the street curb, or eat her words. She sat.

A car approached, horn blaring. Simultaneously, a man leaned his head out a car window to whistle. The next car's driver yelled, "Yo, Mama!" and waved, his Cadillac swerving.

Tom grabbed Blythe from the curb, righted her, then shoved her down the sidewalk. "What the hell were you doing, trying to commit suicide?"

"Using my powers of persuasion, that's what." A gust of unseasonable wind hiked up her hem. She held it down. "I couldn't get you to stop."

"Well, I'm stopped."

The limousine cruised by to her left and wheeled into the parking lot of an Art Deco diner. "Let's get in the car, Tom. We're making a public spectacle of ourselves."

He shook his head. "We've gone as far as we're going."

The finality in his tone caused her heart to miss a beat.

"I don't want you anymore, Redd."

The world stood still. Her heart missed another beat. He'd said many things during their teenage years and lately to prove otherwise. "You're not telling the truth," she choked. "You said you love me. You asked for marriage."

"I asked before I thought everything through. I don't want to spend the rest of my life with you. Can't you understand, Redd? Love doesn't always mean forever."

"I need to sit down." Blythe eyed a bus bench across Broadway, in front of a Chinese restaurant. Barely giving a left-right glance to the street, much less a backward glance at her unappealing hero, she crossed it.

It almost wouldn't have mattered if a bus had hit her.

"Damn fool woman's going to get her neck broken."

Tom followed Blythe to the other side of Broadway, although a neon-hued low-rider nearly socked him. He took the opposite end of the bus bench, his knees making a vee, his forearms settling on thighs, his laced fingers dropping. Tipping his jaw toward her, he said, "It's best we make a clean break."

"Why?"

"I'm not what you need, not for the long haul. You need flash and dash, not some deadbeat Texan who did you wrong. Who'll do you wrong again, by chaining you down."

"I wish you wouldn't tell me what I need."

She scooted along the bench to where her knee touched him. Her eyes glistened. "I need you to love me. As I love you. I love you, Tom!"

He glanced away, unable to meet her eyes. Why? Why *now* did she say those three special words? They made it all the more difficult to let her go. But he must. For her sake.

"Your place isn't with me. You belong to the world." He swallowed. "Go back to it."

"My place is with you. We belong together. Building Phoenix Center and a future. I won't leave you, Tom. I'll resign from Partners in Crisis. I'll devote my life to you and your causes. Just don't send me away."

How would she feel about those sacrifices, somewhere down the line? Lousy, he knew. He shoved to stand. Fingers poking into the back pockets of his jeans, he studied the asphalt pavement rather than the face most beloved to him. He had to hurt her, had to make her understand just how serious he was.

"You need to understand," he said. "It's time for you to move on. I don't want you in on Phoenix Center. You've intruded as far as I'm going to let you."

"Intruded?" she echoed, her voice incredibly small.

"I didn't ask for you to turn up. You showed up. If I'd wanted you back, I would have found you."

"You're lying."

"No. I'm not."

Deserving the punishment of watching countless emotions sweep across her beautiful round features, he made himself look at her. Was this how he'd remember her, when he vegetated on the porch, old and lonely?

"We belonged together as kids," he said, aching worse than his worst day in the hospital. "You went on to a fulfilling life, one that still tempts you. I went on to Dana."

"You're not with her now."

"But I was."

Tears glistened in Blythe's eyes. "You promised… At

the Aztec Motel you promised never to make me cry again.''

Tom looked away, on the verge of giving in to his selfish hunger to keep her with him.

The wheels of a maroon Honda screeched up to the bus bench, a fellow in a Texas Aggies cap stretching his neck toward them. ''You folks know how to get to the zoo?''

''No!'' both Tom and Blythe shouted.

''Excuse me for asking.'' He backed up, roared away.

Blythe's eyes were no longer teary. Anger was now roaring in that sweet round face. She bounced to her feet. ''You're pitiful, Tom, you know that? Plain pitiful, dredging up the past. You live too much in it.''

''How can anyone understand the present, if he doesn't reckon with his history?''

''If you're looking for me to say 'it doesn't matter, the way you dumped me,' I can do that. It doesn't matter that you dumped me. You want me to take your name? I'll do it. Sounds nice. Blythe Tillman.''

Damn—why didn't she stop? How much could he take, hearing everything he'd ever wanted to hear? ''You don't call yourself Mrs. Ricard,'' he said, for lack of any good argument.

She looked down at her hand. ''This is the reason you're upset, isn't it? This ring. You think I'm still in love with Jean-Pierre. I loved him. Not as much as I love you, though. I can't explain why I've kept it on, except to say I should've put it away before I returned to the ranch.'' Slipping off that wedding band and shoving it into her purse, she said, ''I made a mistake. Forgive me.''

The ring hadn't bothered Tom, not lately anyway. He knew she loved him, and knew she respected her late husband's memory. If it were only so simple as jealousy over a circle of diamonds!

How could he get it across that by sacrificing for Blythe, he would give her a gift more precious than jewels? He'd give her the freedom to be herself.

He didn't want to sound self-sacrificing. He knew she'd sacrifice her own life for his happiness. Forcing every bit of grit he could muster, he said coldly, "I want you out of my life. Now and for always."

He studied the intensity of her green eyes, the hurt in every aspect of her bodily stance. He yearned to accept her statements and get back in that vulgar black tank for the trip home, where they would live happily ever after. But they wouldn't.

A saying came to him. It went on the order of—*if you set a bird free and it flies back to you, then it's truly yours.* Blather. Blythe had returned once. No. Twice. The cage he proffered lacked the gilding of excitement.

"You just don't get it, do you, Redd? We made our choices a long time ago. I could've eloped with you, could've flown to Germany. I didn't. You could've not left. You did. You decided what you wanted. You chose a career and a foreign life-style that didn't have to do with cowboys or home on the range."

"You're right, I did." Her glare changed from hot to cool. "But then, you were always somebody else's hero. You were kind to kids, and still are. You were a good neighbor, and a fine son and grandson. You wore a white hat, wore it well. You would have even sacrificed your life to save a kitty. But..." Her voice elevated. "What in the hell do you do for *me!*"

She pivoted to cross the street, not turning her head.

Losing the nerve that had taken last night and this day to gather, he rushed forward, following her into the busy street. "Where are you going?"

Two cars braked when she ground to a halt, midway to the limo. Horns blared; people yelled and made rude gestures.

She whirled back to Tom, giving in to what he asked for. Breaking his heart. "Where am I going?" she said. "The smart place. For an Egyptian body wrap."

"What?"

"Where do you think I'm going? I'm going to Africa."

Africa. Guns. Diseases. If he were with her, he could protect her. Or try to. He made a move of desperation. He grabbed her hand. "Take me with you." Reason surfaced. He couldn't stand by and watch her fall.

"Forget I said that. I don't belong in your world any more than you belong in mine."

"No joke. Where I'm going takes iron guts."

She dashed for the limousine. Yearning to touch her, Tom caught up, just as the chauffeur opened the rear door for her.

Climbing into the limousine, she instructed the driver, "To the airport."

An electric window whirred downward. She popped her head outside. "I forgot something."

Blythe uttered one word as the big black tank rolled away, a word that echoed in Tom's head, settled in his broken heart. And branded his memory.

"*Sayonara.*"

Chapter Thirteen

Blythe returned to Partners in Crisis. Returned with her usual vocational zeal, yet she lacked personal enthusiasm over the next few weeks. She hurt. Hurt as if she'd been stabbed with a thousand daggers, lanced by a thousand spears. It was innumerably more difficult, putting Tom out of mind a third time.

She couldn't.

But she did try. Work helped. It also helped to recall just how heartless he'd been, sending her away.

She took care of loose threads in their relationship. Through Sir Montgomery Honeybone's London connections, she hired a barrister to send an international cashier's check for Pickles's care and feeding.

Along with those instructions went a Power of Attorney to Mr. Thomas Tillman, granting authority to sell the Porsche. The cover letter stated Blythe's wishes.

Funds from the sale were to be used for the enrichment of Phoenix Center.

She didn't mind losing the car. She'd left better things behind, such as her heart.

When the relief mission left Africa in September, she couldn't bring herself to return to Florida. She went with her co-workers to London. She was miserable. At least in Mbotswaka, she'd been able to occupy her time with the sick and suffering. Cold comfort.

Over pre-teatime pints of Guinness in a pub near Westminster Abbey, Blythe sat opposite Sir Monty at a small table of walnut. They sipped ale.

He jacked up a brow in the very English fashion. "I say, I'm told a bundle of letters from Texas caught up with you."

His was a nosy comment, but she'd had no one to confide in, except for the middle-aged nobleman. He'd become her sounding board. She needed to unload, since not one word had she received from Sweet Creek Ranch.

"One letter was from California," she said.

"From that peculiar little lady?"

"You mean, Myrtle Tillman? Yes, I heard from her."

It hadn't escaped notice—the information superhighway of Margaret Saldivar hadn't reached Blythe. Oh, well. Too much China Grove news, especially if it included a Tom report, might set her back immeasurably.

Infusing a positive note, Blythe commented, "I was impressed with Myrtle's writing skills."

"Do tell what she had to say."

"Oliver Rockford gave her a part in one of his films. Shooting begins Christmas. And she's gotten work in a

TV commercial, selling tacos. She's relishing her big-shot status.''

"How quaint."

"Myrtle sent a photograph. She's standing, quite proudly I might add, in front of a new Chevy convertible. Had a Hollywood landmark as backdrop. An oily-looking swain, some years her junior, had his arm draped around her shoulders. I believe his name is Rex.''

"My, my. A serious romance afloat?''

Blythe ran a finger along the condensation on the outside of her mug of Guinness. "Myrtle says she's turned into a real 'chick.' She was always that. You know, she didn't mention Zen.''

"Did she mention her grandson?''

"Not a word." Blythe's fingers tightened on the mug's handle. She blinked away the tears that threatened to fall. Shelly's letter had mentioned Tom, in a round-about way.

"Did the young lady enjoy her summer holiday?''

"She had a great time, going the tourist route. Shelly's back in China Grove. She wants to study journalism in college. Getting an education will take years, of course. Who knows what'll happen in the interim? But Icky's back in the picture. He's turned into a decent sort." Blythe drained her glass.

"Really, you must stop thinking about those two. It's bad for your nerves.''

True, but… "Shelly says Icky's volunteering with the carpentry work at Phoenix Center, when he's not at his computer job in San Antonio. The center will open soon. Margaret's working as Tom's secretary. My guy…'' He wasn't her guy. "Tom is again the town hero.''

If not for her prodding, Tom might still be a pecan-lobbing hermit. That he'd seen his dream to fruition, she couldn't take credit for. He'd done that on his own. Too bad he'd failed as a personal hero.

"Apparently the town is backing Tom with the center," she said. "And kids participate in the building efforts."

"Capital." Sir Monty licked off his ale mustache. "And how does your chap fair?"

She studied her emptied glass. "I don't know. Shelly didn't say."

"You should forget him."

"Easier said than done," she replied, the awful tinkle of loss within her.

"Then you should make one of two choices. Return to Texas and make another bid for the bounder. Or return to Mbotswaka. Now that the local henchman is dead and politics are more stable, we should set up a nursing school to teach the locals how to care for their own."

All her professional life, Blythe had dodged bullets and patched wounds. Never had she been given the opportunity to make a difference in an underdeveloped country after the fighting had ended. As she'd once mentioned to Myrtle, if she taught a man to fish, she could feed him for life.

Big Ben, several blocks in the distance, bonged to announce four in the afternoon. Teatime. The moment the clock rang, several Londoners piled into the pub. Blythe reached a decision.

Her eyes on Sir Monty, she said, "When do we take off?"

* * *

Strange, how emotions could soar to the heights yet lick the ground in despair at the same time. Tom gained personal satisfaction, working with the youth of China Grove. Like Blythe, he'd found his life's work. Too bad he had to contend with a vacant space in his chest, a void that grew with each passing hour.

Suffering for the cause of Blythe Redd was hell.

He heard a crinkling, a candy wrapper being crushed. Sitting at her desk, with Nippy in a basket beside her, in the office of Phoenix Center was Margaret. Not long after Blythe took off for another continent, he'd offered Big Mouth a job. He'd figured it was better to be on her good side, than to have her tongue wagging against him. He now valued her friendship.

"I'm miserable," he admitted, voicing his troubles for the first time. "I love what I'm doing for the kids, but—"

"Everyone in town loves what you're doing with Phoenix Center."

Tom went to the fridge for a can of Ensuromedic, chugged it. "I don't want praise." *I want Redd.*

Margaret punched the CD player's On button, the same boom box that Granny Myrt had bought as a gift. Was it happenstance, hearing the olden day's voice of Billie Holiday? If any singer could wrench Tom into a worse mood, it was Lady Day.

Could be because of her yearning voice. Hers was the voice of a person tortured by losing out on love.

Margaret, meanwhile, attended a computer keyboard; the printer spat a report. "Only two more shopping days till Myrtle hauls her new travel trailer onto the ranch."

Granny Myrt, flush with success, would be here for a

visit. At the party to be attended by staff, board of directors and town kids, Tom planned to ask her to become a member of the board. What started as a goodwill gesture on his part had snowballed, with several prominent business people in San Antonio agreeing to sit the board. Hollywood pizzazz would dress up the council.

Already her TV commercial had run.

"I doubt she'll be keen on the way you mope around, just because you've lost Blythe."

Nippy toddled toward the door. Tom picked the Pomeranian up, scratched his underchin. Lady Day started singing about locking up a heart and throwing away the key.

Margaret sniffed. "If you can't give, and if Blythe can't give, then you must get on with it."

She might be the biggest mouth in town, but she spoke the truth.

"Got to put Redd out of mind." Too bad it hurt worse than a burn, the effort to forget Blythe.

"Like I've told you a zillion times, you need to find out what's in Blythe's mind. She may want you back. Under conditions. Maybe not with conditions. How will you know, unless you ask her?"

"If she turned up, I'd ask her."

"She's turned up twice. How many times must she show her love? When are you going to show yours?"

"Leave me alone."

Margaret could never leave anything alone. "If you'd get yourself together, you and Blythe would make a great team."

Damn. Lady Day, cupped trumpets as her backup,

started singing about lonely days and crying for lost love. "Body and Soul" was her song.

"I'm all for you, body and soul," sang the blues singer.

Just what he needed, a song about love making life hell. He needed to get his mind right. It didn't have anything to do with kissing anyone's grits, or being smart enough not to wear baggy shorts, or anything about spouting lousy poetry, as Blythe had once suggested he do.

This was about getting real.

He was no international celebrity. Never would be. His destiny was tied to China Grove. Blythe might be too large to live the small life, but she'd been willing to give it a try. More than he'd been able to give her.

"I wronged my Redd."

"I hear she's working at a hospital in Mbotswaka, teaching young African women how to be nurses."

As usual, he brooded. That hellhole of a republic might not be as dangerous as it had been, but she could still get hurt.

Margaret contemplated a row of candy bars, lifting one to study it. "Seems to me you guys could hit a happy medium."

"I'd gladly surrender myself to you…body and soul."

Tom listened to Lady Day's voice, her words, and wondered, What did it truly mean, to give and accept body and soul?

"Shut that thing off," he demanded. When Margaret did, he asked, "What have you heard from Redd?"

"Only what Shelly tells. Blythe hasn't written to me.

I haven't written to her. I've done enough meddling in your business."

"Dammit, Margaret. Why stop *now?*"

"If you two are going to work it out, you'll have to do it on your own." Her teeth flashed. "I will say I think you drink Ensuromedic and keep up your exercises, just in case you need to impress her."

"I do it for myself," he said honestly.

Grabbing more papers that belched from the printer, Margaret tamped first the long edges, then the short ones on her desk. "Prudence Packard checked with a travel agent. You can take an Air France flight from Houston to Paris. You could get a nonstop flight from there to Mbotswaka."

"I'm not going to Africa."

"Suit yourself."

"What would I do once I got there?"

Margaret gave strict attention to a Mars candy bar. She peeled one side of the wrapper, then the other. Careful fingers set the paper in the trash. She used a letter opener to split the sweet in two.

"Margaret Saldivar, you've never been laconic, not an hour in your life. I'm going to wring your skinny neck if you don't talk."

Her mischievous eyes were now trained on Tom. "Any fellow who can get a baseball scholarship, be heroic in fires and out, then turn an old beat-up barn into the best thing that ever happened to China Grove—gee, I dunno. Surely you can come up with something."

"Do something!" Blythe yelled in French and glared at a transport driver. The native had chosen to yammer

with one of her prettier students, rather than to unload
his truck of medical supplies. "Don't simply stand
there—move."

The driver moved. Slowly. Lifting her hand that held
a clipboard, Blythe used the back of her fingers to brush
a lock of overlong, dirty bangs from her eyes. She
needed a haircut. In the greater scheme of things, the
condition of her hair had no significance.

The state of her heart? Lousy. She still yearned for
Tom, still ached for him and probably always would.
Don't think about him. He'd called the shots. She must
live with them.

She eyed her classroom of sorts. A tent set up on the
arid planes of central Africa. It wasn't perfect. There was
never enough water, never enough supplies. And each
day brought lines of desperate people needing medical
care.

Another truck came barreling up the dirt path that
served as a road to the tent hospital.

She went to the crates being stacked on the ground,
her intention to check the cargo manifest. Just as a helper
had opened the first box and she'd begun to check the
contents, that mysterious truck braked to a halt between
her and the hospital.

"*Bwana, bwana,*" cried several of the natives, as if
they'd seen a savior.

Desert mirages could play on the mind, but she'd
swear that looked like Tom alighting from the truck's
passenger side, placing a duffel bag on the dusty ground.
Couldn't be.

This Western-hatted man—tanned, sunshades-bedecked
and loaded down with a backpack—wore a short-sleeved-

yoked shirt, but he weighed a good twenty pounds more than the Terrible Tom she'd left in Texas.

As if the man were a messiah, a throng surrounded him.

"I've seen it all now." Her American helper, a fellow from Illinois, twisted his lips. "A cowpoke on the Equator."

"That's no cowpoke. That's my hero!"

The clipboard dropped. Without studying the whys or the what-fors, she ran forward, shoving her way through the crowd and straight to Tom's arms. Her gales of joyful laughter mixed with his as he lifted her off her feet, swinging her around.

Cheers rose from students and workers as well as the others who were able to catch the drift. There was a round of applause. Her helper whistled.

"Hello, pussycat," her hero drawled.

Once he let her slide to stand, she decided to get something straight, even if her forming assumptions at his presence were entirely wrong. "I love you. I've always loved you. I'll always love you. I'm thrilled you're here. But what in the name of insanity are you doing?"

"Can I take back my hateful words?"

"I've forgotten them already."

He smiled. "Granny Myrt sends her love. She's back in Texas to stay. Just got back. Said she'd had enough of California, didn't cotton to Zen and missed playing dominoes. She's going to open her house in town and live in it."

While Blythe ate up the information about her favorite kooky senior citizen, she knew Tom hadn't traveled halfway around the globe to report on his grandmother.

Curious, she asked, "What about her boyfriend?"

"He'll be cutting hair at Kurleen's."

"All right, 'fess up. What are you doing here?"

"Delivering relief supplies. Clothes, food. I got the kids in China Grove in on asking for donations. They did car washes and had a bake sale, too. Which didn't add to much, but I made up the difference."

"That's…that's wonderful." Somehow it didn't surprise Blythe, his launching a relief effort. He'd gone into a burning mobile home for a kitty. No, bringing supplies wasn't an anomaly. It was totally her Tom.

"Bwana! Bwana!"

He took her elbows. Even his bad hand took one. "Is there any place we can talk in private?"

She motioned to the supply tent. "Over there."

Holding hands, they went inside. He tossed sunshades and Stetson aside, unwound his backpack. Sitting on a crate beside him, she strung question after question together, making little sense of any of it, but wanting to know everything about him, especially his purposes.

"Settle down," he said with a grin. "Give me a chance to answer."

She took a calming breath. Most people considered this a hot day. He was sweating, probably thirsty.

"Can't offer coffee or any niceties—we ration water." She swept her hand to indicate the tent. "This is as good as it gets." She dug in her pocket. "But I have a couple peppermints. Want one?"

Devilment in those wonderful blue eyes, he freed one bonbon from its wrapper, popped it in his perfect mouth, then opened the backpack. "I have a gift for you. Brought it all the way from Gay Paree."

"Imagine that... Tom Tillman in Paris." Her eyes were moist with tears of happiness. "Tom Tillman in Mbotswaka, bearing gifts."

"You'll like this gift." He pulled out a boxlike something from his gear. "Champagne. Good stuff. French." He unwrapped a bottle packed in dry ice. "Shall we toast?"

"What are we toasting?"

"My wising up." He took her hand, lacing their fingers together. "I had a hard time accepting your dedication to all this." He nodded at the tent. "But I realized, when you love someone, it's body and soul. Your soul is here, just like mine's with Phoenix Center. What I'm wanting to do is offer you a deal." He clammed up.

"Tom, talk! You know I can't stand a mystery."

"I believe in you. I'm not crazy about bullets, but then, neither are you. You just keep climbing mountains and molehills, sweet'eart, so you can stay in shape to dodge bullets."

"I can do that," she said, her heart pounding.

"I'll stand behind your causes, if you'll stand behind mine. You go ahead and teach nursing. You follow Partners in Crime, wherever they take you."

"Crisis. Partners in Crisis."

"Partners in Crisis," he corrected. "But when they don't need you, I want you home with me. At the ranch. Will you marry me?"

Had she heard right? A proposal strung together with explanations? Who cared?

He popped the champagne's cork; it bounced off the top of the tent. "Well? Do you think you could get away from here long enough for a honeymoon at the Georges Cinq?"

"The smartest thing I ever did in my life was taking a chance on you, Tom Tillman." She jumped onto his lap, squeezing him tightly, being squeezed in return, ready for the wonderful partnership of their marriage. "You are terrific!"

"Is that a yes?"

"Yes!"

Life could be very, very sweet. Even on the African veld. Even in a town called China Grove. Life was sweet.

* * * * *

Silhouette ® SPECIAL EDITION ®

Newfound sisters Bliss, Tiffany and Katie
learn more about family and true love
than they *ever* expected.

A new miniseries by
LISA JACKSON

A FAMILY KIND OF GUY (SE#1191) August 1998
Bliss Cawthorne wanted nothing to do with ex-flame
Mason Lafferty, the cowboy who had destroyed her
dreams of being his bride. Could Bliss withstand his irresistible charm—the second time around?

A FAMILY KIND OF GAL (SE#1207) November 1998
How could widowed single mother Tiffany Santini be
attracted to her sexy brother-in-law, J.D.? Especially
since J.D. was hiding something that could destroy the
love she had just found in his arms....

And watch for the conclusion of this series in
early 1999 with Katie Kinkaid's story in
A FAMILY KIND OF WEDDING.

Available at your favorite retail outlet. Only from

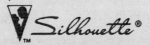

MEN at WORK

All work and no play?
Not these men!

July 1998
MACKENZIE'S LADY by Dallas Schulze
Undercover agent Mackenzie Donahue's
lazy smile and deep blue eyes were his best
weapons. But after rescuing—and kissing!—
damsel in distress Holly Reynolds, how could
he betray her by spying on her brother?

August 1998
MISS LIZ'S PASSION by Sherryl Woods
Todd Lewis could put up a building with ease,
but quailed at the sight of a classroom! Still,
Liz Gentry, his son's teacher, was no battle-ax,
and soon Todd started planning some
extracurricular activities of his own....

September 1998
A CLASSIC ENCOUNTER
by Emilie Richards
Doctor Chris Matthews was intelligent, sexy
and *very* good with his hands—which made
him all the more dangerous to single mom
Lizette St. Hilaire. So how long could she
resist Chris's special brand of TLC?

Available at your favorite retail outlet!

MEN AT WORK™

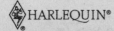 

Look us up on-line at: http://www.romance.net

PMAW2

 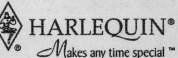